The Experiment

Behind the desk, with his back to the door, sat a figure. A figure with black hair and a silver streak, the thin string of an eye patch tied in the back.

Professor DeLure.

Caryl stood for a long moment watching him. Clearing her throat nervously, she spoke at last. "Professor DeLure?"

The Professor stayed motionless for an instant longer. Then, deliberately, he swung his chair around to face Caryl.

Her lips parted. She felt her heart beat faster. She'd never looked directly into his face before. His gaze was hypnotic, mesmerizing.

For a moment he just stared. Then his whole expression underwent a horrifying transformation...

NIGHTMARE HALL

The Experiment

Diane Hoh

■ SCHOLASTIC

Scholastic Children's Books,
Commonwealth House, 1–19 New Oxford Street,
London WC1A 1NU, UK
a division of Scholastic Ltd
London~New York~Toronto~Sydney~Auckland

First published in the US by Scholastic Inc., 1994
First published in the UK by Scholastic Ltd, 1996

Copyright © Nola Thacker, 1994

ISBN 0 590 13380 2

Printed by Cox and Wyman Ltd, Reading, Berks

10 9 8 7 6 5 4 3 2

Prologue

"Beautiful," he murmured. "You are beautiful."

She didn't answer. She ignored him. She stroked her silky hair and thought, perhaps, about dinner.

The Professor smiled ruefully.

He was used to being admired. Responded to. Accustomed to being noticed, most especially by the females of the species.

Maybe that's why he liked her so much.

She'd led a sheltered life. She'd never even been in his office before. Very few ever had.

Now she sat in the window, indifferent to the view, indifferent to the singular honor accorded her by the Professor's attentions, an honor that any other female at Salem University would have, possibly, killed for.

Not that she wasn't a killer. She was. It was one of the things that made him so attracted to her. So morbidly attracted to her.

He leaned toward her slightly.

She froze. Then she hissed.

The Professor laughed softly. "Ah, my pretty, I could crush you. Don't you know that?"

She didn't answer.

He didn't move.

They stayed like that, each watching the other, waiting, two predators.

So intent were they on their perverse courtship that they were unaware of a third observer standing just outside the partially open office door.

A third predator.

Watching.

Waiting.

All of them were deadly.

Only one of them could win.

But only time would tell who would live and who would die:

The observer.

The Professor.

Or the spider.

Chapter 1

"He's a killer."

"Wrong," said Caryl.

"And you're crazy."

"Wrong again," Caryl said, keeping her eyes fixed on the massive oak doors of Griswold Hall.

"Caryl Elizabeth Amberly!" said Anna Singh. "Are you listening to me?"

"He's a killer and I'm crazy," repeated Caryl. Her face broke into a smile. "Killer handsome and I'm crazy about him. There he is!"

The massive glass doors of Griswold Hall opened and a dark, striking older man emerged and paused at the top of the flagstone steps as if he couldn't quite remember how he'd gotten there.

"I don't believe this," muttered Anna.

Caryl didn't answer her best friend at all this time. She kept her gaze fastened on Professor Maximillian DeLure, biology professor at Salem University, and poet, as he began to walk slowly down the front steps of Griswold.

The Professor didn't seem to notice the two first-year Salem students who sat on the bench at the foot of the stairs. His head was bowed as if he were deep in thought. The single lock of silver that streaked his black hair had tumbled across his forehead and he brushed it back impatiently with one pale, slender-fingered hand as he passed. His appearance was made even more memorable by the black patch that covered one eye. His height, his dark coloring, the intensity that emanated from him, all added to his aura of mystery and allure. And *danger*.

Even though she'd never had a single class with Professor DeLure, Caryl Elizabeth Amberly, first-year student and aspiring writer, was more than half in love with him. And she was not the only one on the Salem University campus.

At the foot of the stairs the Professor turned, still without looking up, and walked slowly away across the carefully manicured grass in the direction of the student center.

"Isn't he incredible?" said Caryl.

"Killer incredible," agreed Anna sarcastically.

Caryl turned, flushing slightly, a flash of annoyance in her golden brown eyes. "You know, sometimes I wonder, Anna, how we stay friends. You might at least be a little understanding about my feelings."

Anna's own, darker brown eyes met Caryl's steadily. "I do understand. You've got a massive crush on the Prince of Evil. And I'm not just talking about what everyone else says about him . . ."

"Oh, that." Caryl made an impatient gesture. "Not everyone believes *gossip*, you know."

"That's why I said I wasn't just talking about what other people said. I'd also like to point out that taking one — just one — of any of his classes will convince you that Professor De-Lure is out to kill the students. I mean, the homework alone. Ugh."

"Anna! That's what we're here for, right? An education?"

"Puh-leeze," said Anna.

Just then the massive doors opened again, this time slamming backwards so hard that it seemed as if they were going to be torn from their hinges. "Professor!" a voice called, and an athletic-looking guy dressed in ripped jeans and a sweatshirt sporting a huge bleach mark on the shoulder came bounding down the stairs.

"Nicholas!" said Anna, her voice changing so

much that Caryl looked at her in surprise.

The boy stopped. "Oh. Ahh — Anna, right?"

"Intro Zoology," Anna supplied, smiling cheerfully, as if it were her favorite class on earth.

Carly's mouth dropped open at Anna's sudden change of behavior, as Nicholas answered perfunctorily, "Oh. Yeah, right. How're you doing?"

"Super. Nicholas, this is my friend Caryl. Caryl, Nicholas France. He's Professor De-Lure's student assistant."

"You are?" said Caryl. "Do you know anything about his new seminar? Experiment: Poets and Scientists? I tried out for it and . . ." Her voice trailed off. Nicholas, who'd been about to turn away even as Anna was introducing Caryl, had suddenly stopped. Now he stared down at Caryl intently. His eyes were a mesmerizing blue, oddly at variance with his laid-back appearance. Caryl noticed a tiny white scar at the edge of his hairline near his ear.

I wonder what happened, she thought irrelevantly.

"Uh, Nicholas?" said Anna. "Is everything okay?"

With what seemed like an effort, Nicholas tore his attention away from Caryl. "Sorry," he said. He turned back to Caryl. "I was . . . you reminded me of someone . . ."

Caryl laughed. "Someone you like, I hope."

"Sure," said Nicholas. Abruptly changing the subject, he focused his attention on Anna, almost pointedly ignoring Caryl. "The Poets and Scientists seminar. Did you try out for it, Anna? The notices about who made it went out in the campus mail yesterday afternoon. People should be getting them today."

"No," said Anna.

"Oh. Well, I have to go," said Nicholas. "I need to catch the Prof. See you guys later."

"See you, Nick," Anna called after him.

"What a weirdo," said Caryl, frowning.

"Not as weird as some of the guys *you* go out with," said Anna.

"You can't judge a book by the cover," retorted Caryl.

"Yeah, but you can at least be a little picky about what you read."

"I walk the straight, but not the narrow." Caryl grinned at Anna. Then Nicholas's last words suddenly registered. Caryl grabbed Anna's arm. "Did you hear that? What Nicholas said?"

Anna groaned. "I was hoping you didn't."

"Anna! The notices about who made it into

Professor's DeLure's class are probably in the mailboxes *right now*. Let's go!"

"So what do you think of Nicholas?" asked Anna, allowing Caryl to pull her in the direction of the student union post office.

"Nicholas? He's okay."

"Okay? Are you kidding? He's got gorgeous eyes!"

Remembering Nicholas's strangely unsettling stare, Caryl made a face. She opened her mouth to say something flip — but then she saw the look on Anna's face. *Anna* has a crush on Nicholas France, Caryl realized. Serious, practical Anna!

She grinned. "Oooh, Anna," she said and Anna turned bright red.

"C'mon," Anna said, before Caryl could say anything else. "Let's go. I thought you were in a hurry to get to the PO."

The Salem U post office, tucked snugly in the bottom rear of the student union, was as quaint and traditional as most of the rest of the Salem campus. The huge, ornate old bronze-colored mailboxes with their double combination locks lined a narrow maze of aisles to one side of the stamp and package windows near the entrance. Anna's mailbox was near the windows, and she stopped to check her mail while

Caryl hurried toward her own mailbox in the back of the post office.

There it was. Last aisle, lower right-hand back corner. Salem University Substation PO Box 315. Caryl bent forward, trying, in vain as usual, to see through the thick little window of glass.

This is it, she thought. With nerveless fingers, she twirled the double locks. Slowly, she pulled the door open. She reached inside.

Then leaped back and began to scream.

Chapter 2

"Ahhhhhhhhhh!"

Caryl stumbled backwards, dropping her pack, as Anna came running toward her.

"Caryl! Are you okay? What is — eeek!"

Anna leaped back, too, as a hand emerged from Caryl's open mailbox, wriggling its fingers.

"Oooooooooooh," a voice intoned. "It's the ghost of number 315."

"Ben Cage!" exclaimed Caryl in outrage, her cheeks flaming. "You, you . . . you immature hormone bucket!"

The hand withdrew. "Hey," said an aggrieved voice. "It was just a *joke!*"

"Just a joke? The whole post office is staring at me!" Caryl looked up and realized that it was true. She also realized that one of the reasons people were staring now was because she was leaning over to shout into a mailbox.

"Ben," she said, lowering her voice. "Where's my mail?"

There was no answer. "Ben!" hissed Caryl furiously.

"Special delivery," said a voice behind her. Caryl whirled around as Anna started to snicker.

"Ben Cage, you are in deep trouble!" exclaimed Caryl.

"Even though I brought you your mail personally?" Ben was a slight boy with an unruly mop of reddish hair and a hugely infectious grin, who had a work-study job at the Salem post office. He tried his grin now on Caryl. "I didn't mean to scare you. At least, not much."

"Can I have my mail?" said Caryl, resisting the impulse to grin back.

"If you'll forgive me," said Ben. "And tell me our date's still on."

A little smile crept into Caryl's eyes. Ben *was* sweet — even if he was an immature child next to Professor DeLure. "Of course. Now. My mail?" She held out her hand, palm up.

"It must be important," said Ben, still smiling, but watching her closely.

"It is. The most important thing in my life."

"A love letter?" asked Ben.

Anna snorted.

"Anna, you have no romance in your heart," said Caryl. To Ben she said, "No, it's not a love letter. It's a class notice."

With a flourish, Ben laid a thin envelope on it. "Gotta get back to work. Talk to you later."

Caryl nodded, balancing the envelope on her palm.

"Maybe I'll call you tonight," added Ben as he walked away.

"Okay," said Caryl, barely hearing him. This is it, she thought. This could change my life forever. Funny that such a little thing, an envelope with a piece of paper in it, could carry such weight . . .

"Aren't you going to open it?" asked Anna.

"Yeah. Okay. Here goes." Taking a deep breath, Caryl ripped the envelope open and pulled out the enclosed typewritten sheet.

"Well?" said Anna.

"I'm in!" shrieked Caryl, forgetting that she had ever cared that everyone in the post office was staring at her. She grabbed Anna and whirled her in a mad dance down the aisle. "I'm in, I'm in, I'm in!"

"Hey, hey," Anna said breathlessly. "Congratulations. I think."

"You think! Let's go get some chocolate sin.

My treat. To celebrate. Anything you want. What do you think about that?"

"I think Morte par Chocolat," said Anna promptly, referring to the dessert and coffee bar just off campus.

"You got it. Come on. Oh, Anna, what if I hadn't gotten in? It would have just killed me."

Caryl spun around one more time and began to dance lightly up the stairs and out of the PO.

Behind her, Anna stopped smiling. She answered softly, so softly that Caryl couldn't hear, "No. It's Professor DeLure who's going to kill you . . ."

"A double scoop of vanilla fudge and chocolate chocolate chip with hot fudge, double nuts, double sprinkles, *and* a mocha coffee with whipped cream." Anna handed the menu to the waiter and leaned back, a pleased expression on her face.

"I don't believe it!" Caryl was laughing helplessly.

"Your treat, remember?" said Anna smugly.

The waiter left and the two girls settled back. Morte par Chocolat had the usual lunchtime crowd of students avoiding the cafeteria food in favor of sugar, chocolate, and caffeine. As the waiter returned with Caryl's cappuccino and Anna's mocha coffee, Caryl sighed with satisfaction. If you closed your eyes slightly, you could almost imagine this was Paris and all the students were really poets and writers and artists. Or, if not Paris, maybe San Francisco. Or New York.

And now she was one, too. Oh, maybe not a real poet *yet*. But her poetry had been good enough to get her into Professor DeLure's seminar. Only twelve students chosen, and she was one of them.

"I just *looove* this place." A sweetly sarcastic voice echoed Caryl's thoughts and she turned to see Perri Biddle. "Hi," said Perri, blinking her big cat green eyes at Caryl and Anna.

"Hi, Perri," said Anna unenthusiastically.

Perri flipped her fingers at the waiter. "Double espresso," she cooed. "With a twist." Caryl watched, torn between amusement and disgust, as he practically levitated back to the counter to get Perri's order. How did someone so obviously phoney do it? How did she have that effect on guys?

"So, I just had the most amazing news, children." Perri slid into the empty seat at the little bistro table and pressed her hands together dramatically above her heart. Or where her heart would have been if she'd had one, thought

Caryl, watching what she always thought of as the Perri Act.

As usual, Perri was dressed expensively, but, also as usual, she somehow made it look trashy. Was it that the cashmere sweater was too tight? The little leather skirt just a little too little? Or the way her silver-blonde hair, pulled up in a ponytail on top of her head, tumbled somehow suggestively around her face?

Or was it just the way Perri acted? Like she was her gender's gift to sex?

The waiter reappeared with the espresso. "Thank you ever so," breathed Perri, half-mockingly, and Caryl recognized a line from an old Marilyn Monroe movie. But the waiter didn't seem to. He blushed absurdly and ducked his head and practically bowed as he backed away.

"Perri," said Caryl, unable to stand it any longer. "What do you want?"

Raising the espresso cup, Perri smiled. "I want you to congratulate me, of course. A toast. It's official. Professor DeLure wants — *moi*."

Caryl felt her heart sink as Anna asked, "Wants you? What are you talking about? You're taking one of his Intro Science classes?"

Perri's brows drew together and she shuddered slightly. "Science. Euuww. So gross! Never."

"Then what?" asked Anna.

The little smile on Perri's face made her look more than ever like a cat. "Just because you live on the same hall in the Quad with me, Anna dearest, doesn't mean you know everything about me."

Nothing that can't be read on the bathroom walls, thought Caryl spitefully, but she held her tongue. With a sick feeling, she knew what was coming.

And she was right.

"I made it into Experiment: Poets and Scientists." She paused and sipped delicately at her espresso, watching them over the rim of the cup. Despite her efforts, something of Caryl's chagrin must have shown on her face, because Perri went on in her sweetest, witchiest voice, "Oh, dear. You tried out for that class, too, didn't you, Caryl? I didn't mean to brag. I hope I didn't make you feel too bad. . . ."

Through stiff lips, Caryl said, "About what? As a matter of fact, you'll be in the class with me."

For one satisfying moment, she watched Perri at a loss for words.

But then the waiter came again, all eager

attention, and, staring at Perri, plunked down Anna's sundae and Caryl's piece of chocolate times five cake with coffee ice cream.

"Will there be anything else?" he asked, still staring at Perri.

"No, thank you," said Caryl quickly.

Perri let her eyes travel over the two orders in front of Caryl and Anna and made a rapid recovery. She gave a little snort of laughter. "Wait. Don't tell me. Caryl got into Professor DeLure's class and the two best friends are celebrating. With sweets. Just like the little kids. How — sweet."

Caryl felt her cheeks turn hot with anger, but she wasn't as fast at being mean as Perri. She hadn't had the practice. She watched in speechless fury as Perri pushed her espresso away, dropped a handful of money on the table, and stood up. "See ya in class," she said, before Caryl and Anna could answer. "Have fun with your little party." And then she was gone.

"I hate that bimbo," said Anna.

"She's enough to curdle chocolate," agreed Caryl. They looked at each other and suddenly burst out laughing. Caryl cut a bit of cake and Anna dug out a spoonful of ice cream. Holding their silverware high, they clicked it.

"A toast," said Caryl. "To our little party."

"To science," said Anna.

"To poetry," said Caryl. "And the most interesting semester of our lives."

She didn't know then how prophetic her words were — or how frighteningly interesting her life was about to become.

Chapter 3

What a perfect day, thought Caryl dreamily as she drifted through her afternoon classes. Almost totally perfect. Except for one thing.

Caryl kept thinking of Perri Biddle, fatally attractive Perri Biddle, sitting in Professor DeLure's class. Once Professor DeLure saw Perri, how could he notice any of his other students?

Of course, Perri was no poet. Caryl was sure of that. Perri probably thinks any two words that rhyme are poetry, for pete's sake, thought Caryl. Like night-light. Perri would probably even call that a haiku or something.

So how did Perri get into the class?

Had the Professor met her before? Was he the kind of guy to be swayed by someone as phoney and obvious as Perri?

Walking slowly back across the campus from her last class, Caryl remembered all that she had heard about Professor DeLure.

Professor Maximillian DeLure, award-winning poet, scientist, and professor at Salem University. Specialist in animal behavior studies.

Mystery man.

Caryl had read his poetry. His poems were dark, intricate puzzles, full of pain and violent images, the fabric of nightmares.

She'd also looked up an article he'd written for a scientific journal about the Sherlock Holmes story "The Hound of the Baskervilles," about an evil ghost dog who was haunting and killing a family. Professor DeLure's article had been neither dark and frightening, nor scientifically dry, but an almost lighthearted speculation on what kind of dog the Hound of the Baskervilles might have been and what could have made it behave the way it had.

Caryl didn't like science, but she'd been absorbed by the writing.

And by how different it was from his poetry.

As if he were two different people.

She stopped and stared in the direction of Griswold Hall.

He wasn't married. Didn't have children. But behind those facts were a host of rumors: that he'd been married once; that he'd had a child; that he'd killed them both and now made his poetry from their murders; that the clues to the supposed killings, never solved, were somehow contained in his poems.

She'd also heard that he'd never had children; that he'd driven his wife mad and she was in a mental institution; that she'd put out his eye attempting to escape from him . . .

"Phooey," Caryl said aloud. She didn't believe a word of it. No. A truly sensitive person could tell by looking that the professor was no murderer, no madman — except, of course, in the way great poets were supposed to be mad.

And undoubtedly he'd suffered, suffered still, from some secret tragedy too private for the world to know.

He was alone. Alone and misunderstood. No one could understand him. Maybe no one had really tried.

Except her.

With sudden resolution, Caryl turned in the direction of Griswold Hall. She was going to Professor DeLure's office. She'd see if he was there, introduce herself. Tell him how much she was looking forward to starting his class next Monday.

It couldn't hurt. Could it?

As Caryl cut through the topiary garden, the ongoing Botany for Sculptors project next to

Griswold Hall, the shadows there made all the figures look a little spooky. Professor DeLure, she remembered suddenly, had written a poem about a topiary creature. One that had come to life . . .

She shook off the sudden feeling of unease and hurried up the front steps of Griswold and into the entrance hall. Inside, she stopped. Where was the Professor's office? She'd never actually been in the science building before.

She'd never had a reason to be.

Ah, good. She spotted a directory. The top floor. All the science faculty offices must be there. Taking a deep breath for courage, she walked purposefully up the stairs.

With the last class period of the day over until the evening, the building was quiet. Caryl's footsteps echoed on the polished oak floors as she reached the top of the stairs on the fourth floor and turned down the hall. For a moment she was tempted to call out, to see if anyone answered. But what would she say? Hello? Anybody home? That would be stupid.

She walked on unspeaking, past the unfamiliar names of the science professors, through the unfamiliar smells of the science building. She had never liked science, even though she had been good at it. She liked math better. It seemed less bloody, more exact, somehow. In a way, math was like poetry.

She'd never appreciated science at all — until she'd read the Professor's poems.

Caryl reached the end of the hall. On her left was a windowless door with a double deadbolt lock on it. Just past it, on the same side, was an oak door with a frosted window and a simple name plate beneath: M. DeLure.

Yes.

The door was slightly ajar and a thin thread of light shone out into the hall and gave the frosted glass a ghostly glow.

Caryl raised her hand and knocked softly.

No one answered.

She hesitated. Should she knock again? Suppose he was involved in one of his poems? Immersed in it? What if she interrupted him, ruined his creative vision?

Not only would he hate her forever, but she'd probably flunk his course.

Get a grip, Caryl, she told herself.

She knocked again, slightly louder.

No answer.

At last, hesitantly, she put her hand on the door and pushed it carefully open.

A spacious, but very crowded corner office met her eyes. A green glass-shaded lamp on a battered oak desk by the window at the far end of the office shed a golden light. In the shadows beyond the lamp's rays, oak file cabinets lined one wall. Above the file cabinets were bookshelves crammed with books and magazines and papers. A scuffed leather chair was crammed into a far corner beneath a battered floor lamp. In the other corner was a closed door with a curiously wrought brass handle. Through the mullioned windows the campus glowed dark green, and glinted with lights from the windows of other buildings in the early shadows of the evening.

Behind the desk, with his back to the door, staring out at the view, sat a figure. A figure with black hair and a silver streak, the thin string of an eye patch tied in the back.

Professor DeLure.

She stood for a long moment watching him. What was he thinking about?

He seemed so lost. So lonely.

Clearing her throat nervously, Caryl spoke at last. "Professor DeLure?"

The chair shifted slightly, and Caryl saw, past the professor's shoulder, a small aquarium. In it a brilliantly colored red fish with black markings hung suspended in the water. With a savageness made somehow more shocking by its small size and striking beauty, it flung itself against a mirror suspended in the water. Again. And again. And again.

The Professor stayed motionless for an instant longer. Then, deliberately, he swung his chair around to face Caryl.

Her lips parted. She felt her heart beat faster. She'd never looked directly into his face before. His gaze was hypnotic, mesmerizing.

For a moment she forgot everything except the beating of her heart.

What was she there for?

Oh, yes.

"I'm Caryl Amberly. I'm going to be in your new class, Experiment: Poets and — "

"Stop." Professor DeLure's voice was low and penetrating.

She stood for a moment, foolishly, her mouth opened. Then she closed it. His eye was midnight blue, almost the color of violets. For a moment he just stared. Then his whole expression underwent a horrifying transformation, as if he wished he could burn the skin from her face with his eye.

"You!" he exclaimed, his voice harsh. "Who are you?"

"I'm trying to tell you!" she swallowed shakily. I'm imagining this, she thought. Aloud she went on, "I'm going to be one of your students. In Experiment: Poets and Scientists. I'm Caryl

Amberly and it is such an honor . . ."

The red fury of the fish behind the Professor had not abated. Caryl stopped, then said, "Can't you do something? About the fish? It's — it's killing itself."

Abruptly Professor DeLure swiveled the chair around and removed the mirror from the water. The fish stopped fighting instantly and hung motionless, almost corpselike, in the water.

The Professor looked down at the mirror in his hand. "Thus we fight with illusion," he murmured.

He looked up again at Caryl. Involuntarily, she took a step back from the expression in his eye.

"Run, Caryl Amberly, run!" he grated.

"What?" said Caryl.

"Go! Now!"

Mortified, humiliated, Caryl spun around, crashed into the door and staggered. She looked over her shoulder.

Professor DeLure had risen. He seemed to tower above her in the jumbled room.

"RUN!" he thundered.

Blindly Caryl wrenched the door open and obeyed. Without even knowing what she was doing, she ran as fast as she could down the dark corridor toward the stairs, toward freedom. Away from the monster behind her, who had begun to laugh.

"That's right! That's right, my pretty. Run! Run!

"Run for your life!"

Chapter 4

"Crazy! I told you," said Anna.

"Worried about losing your tiny little mind?" Caryl and Anna looked up to see Perri standing in the door of Anna's dorm room.

"Puh-leeze, Perri. Go away. I'm having a bad enough day already," answered Caryl before she could stop herself.

Perri put her hands on her hips and tossed her hair back with a practiced gesture of her head. "So you're having a bad day, Caryl? Professor DeLure tell you it was a mistake, your getting into his class?"

"No," said Caryl shortly.

"Too bad," said Perri, showing her teeth in a phoney smile. She slid away, snakelike, before Caryl could answer.

"What a witch," muttered Anna.

"You won't get any argument from me," said Caryl. "Amazing how she always manages to turn up at the worst possible moment — and make it *worse*."

They were both silent for a moment, then Caryl switched back to the subject at hand. "Professor DeLure is *not* crazy, Anna. There's got to be an explanation for what happened in his office today. A *logical* explanation," she added quickly, seeing Anna's stubborn look.

The two girls, Anna sprawled across her bed and Caryl sitting on the floor propped against the closet door, fell silent again. Around them, the dorm hummed with evening activity: doors slamming, phones ringing, people getting ready for dinner and dates and studying and evening classes. It was hard to believe, listening to the familiar, comforting background noise, that anything as bizarre as what had happened in Professor DeLure's office that afternoon could be possible.

But it was.

Wasn't it?

Still, how could it be?

Caryl sighed deeply.

Anna began twirling a lock of her straight black hair around and around her little finger in a characteristic gesture, her brow furrowed in thought. As last she said, "Okay. Assuming your Professor DeLure — "

"He's not '*my* Professor DeLure!' "

" — is not crazy, and mind you, this is only an assumption for the sake of argument, there are a couple of other explanations."

"Like what, Anna?"

"Like *you're* crazy?" said Anna solemnly.

Caryl knew Anna meant it as a joke, but somehow it didn't feel funny.

She frowned. "I'm not crazy."

"You're crazy about Professor DeLure."

"No, I'm not! I happen to think he is cute . . . okay, no, okay, handsome. I happen to think he is brilliant. I happen to admire his work, okay? That doesn't make me crazy. And just because he's a genius — "

"A genius!" cried Anna indignantly. "I'll tell you what kind of genius he is! The genius of *mean*. Have you had one of his biology tests?"

"A genius," repeated Caryl stubbornly. "But he's not crazy."

"Then maybe you imagined it. I don't mean the whole thing, I mean how it all happened. I mean, think about it, Caryl. The Siamese fighting fish — "

"What?"

"That's what that fish was you described. A male Siamese fighting fish. It'll fight to the death with another fish — or with its own reflection in a mirror.

"You're watching this insane fish, you're all

nervous, about to talk to the teacher of your dreams for the first time, the dim light, the whole bit. It's like a scene from a play, almost. Maybe everything just seemed exaggerated somehow, because of all that."

Caryl thought back over the events. Was it possible? Had she been so nervous, so tense and excited that she'd overreacted?

Suddenly she began to doubt her own judgment. What if she had imagined everything?

What if she'd misinterpreted what had happened? What if Professor DeLure now thought she was some weird, crazy student?

The thought made Caryl squirm inwardly.

She looked up to see Anna watching her intently. "Well?" Anna prodded. "Is it possible your mind was playing a little trick on you, maybe?"

"Maybe," conceded Caryl reluctantly.

"Good," said Anna, jumping up. "Because my stomach is playing tricks on me. Let's go get something to eat, okay?"

"Okay," said Caryl. Getting to her feet, she told herself, *Anna is right.*

Anna had to be right. Or one of them — Professor DeLure, or she, Caryl Elizabeth Amberly — might just be going . . .

Crazy.

* * *

She slipped the towel from her shoulders. The indoor pool at the Robeson Athletic Center was empty. It usually was at that hour. It was why she liked to swim then. To do long, slow laps. It relaxed her somehow. Gave her time to think.

She dove into the pool. The water was colder than she expected. It made her gasp.

Oh, well. Swimming laps would warm her up soon enough.

Stroke, stroke, stroke, breathe.

Stroke, stroke, stroke, breathe.

After awhile she realized that she had been swimming for a long time. She lifted her head. The end of the pool was still a long way away.

Suddenly the pool seemed very big.

Suddenly she began to be afraid.

She put down her head and began to swim faster.

Stroke, stroke, stroke breathestrokestroke-stroke

Something swirled past her in the water.

She stopped abruptly.

She gasped.

An enormous, monstrous creature was coming toward her, its bulging black eyes fixed on her, its blood-red fins churning the water into a gory froth.

She froze for a moment.

And then she heard his voice.

Professor DeLure's voice.

"Swim!" he screamed, and began to laugh insanely. "Swim, my pretty!

"Swim for your life!"

Chapter 5

"No!"

Caryl sat up in bed, gasping for air.

She thought she'd screamed. But she couldn't have. No one had come running to see what was the matter. Her roommate Phyllis's silent form slept on in the bed against the far wall.

The dorm was quiet and still around her.

The only thing she could hear was the frantic beating of her heart.

It was only a dream, she told herself. Only a dream.

A nightmare.

Nightmares weren't real. Nightmares didn't come true.

After a long, long time Caryl lay back down and forced herself to close her eyes. And after a much, much longer time, she fell into a restless, uneasy sleep.

* * *

"Caryl!"

Ben bounded up beside Caryl as she walked across the campus, headed for Griswold Hall. Monday afternoon at last. Time for the first class with Professor DeLure.

"Whoa," said Ben, pretending to reel in shock. "I mean, you look great all the time, but today, it's like, *special*."

Caryl felt her cheeks start to burn with embarrassment. "Thanks," she said, trying to act casual. Maybe she shouldn't have worn a dress. People hardly ever wore dresses to class. But she liked this dress. It made her feel older. Sophisticated.

As if she could handle anything.

As if she could handle whatever might happen in Professor DeLure's class.

She'd never felt so excited and so panicky about anything before, especially a class.

What if the Professor stood up and threw her out of the class?

What if he ignored her completely?

What if she made a complete jerk out of herself, acted like some world-class nerd?

"Caryl? You weren't listening," Ben complained.

"Yes, I was."

"So will you?"

"Will I what?"

Ben rolled his eyes. "Will you go to see *Night of the Living Dead* with me at the Screening Room this Saturday?"

It was Caryl's turn to roll her eyes. "Ben. We went to see *The Fly* this past Saturday. What about something a little less gruesome? I mean, where do you get this obsession with the truly weird and the violent?"

"*The Fly* is a classic! So is *Night of the Living Dead*!" Ben looked so indignant, Caryl had to laugh.

"Okay, okay," she said.

"Great," said Ben. "And next time, *you* can choose the movie."

"Gee, thanks," murmured Caryl. They'd reached Griswold Hall. She stopped at the foot of the stairs and lifted her chin. "See ya," she said to Ben.

He grinned. "All right."

The inside of the building looked considerably different from the way she remembered it. The shadows were gone. Students drifted in and out of the labs and classrooms.

Catching a glimpse of Perri ahead of her, Caryl fell in behind her at a discreet distance and followed her into one of the smaller classrooms at the end of the first floor hall. As unobtrusively as possible, Caryl slid into the first empty seat. Only after she had pulled out her notebook and carefully deposited her pack under her feet did she allow herself to look around the room.

He wasn't there yet. Caryl didn't know whether she was relieved or disappointed. To distract herself, she began to study the other students.

There was Perri, of course. Perri had chosen to wear a dress, too — if a low-wrapped body suit attached to six inches of skirt could be called a dress. Caryl felt almost conservative in her own outfit.

Resolutely, she switched her attention from Perri. On the far side of the room, she recognized one of the senior varsity cheerleaders in his letter jacket. He was talking to one of the star forwards of the basketball team, who was also wearing her letter jacket. And Caryl wasn't sure, but she was almost certain that the guy with his hair pulled back in a long ponytail, scowling down at a book of poems in French, with the word *Baudelaire* on the cover, was Jason Wu, the campus poet and editor of the literary magazine.

And Dare Winters.

Who wouldn't recognize Dare Winters?

He was lounging in one of the chairs near the front, his hands thrust into his pockets, his attention on something outside the window.

Dare Winters, with his blue eyes and black hair. Who would have thought he'd be in her class? She'd never even been that close to him before. But she'd been close enough to know what he did to her heartbeat. Bad, people said. Dare Winters was bad.

Bad and gorgeous.

Of course, Perri had realized Dare was there, too. With characteristic lack of subtlety, she had gotten up from the seat she'd first chosen, near the front, and slid into the seat next to Dare, giving him a blinding smile when he turned her way.

So absorbed was Caryl in the whole scene that she forgot for a moment where she was.

It was at that moment that Professor Maximillian DeLure came striding into the room.

"Hello, boys and girls," he said, lifting the eyebrow above his eyepatch and surveying the room.

The gesture was an unnerving one. The class stared back wordlessly.

Professor DeLure threw back his head and laughed. "But you're not, are you? That's the point, isn't it? You're not boys and girls. You're adults. Poets. Writers. Scientists.

"So hello, colleagues. I'm delighted you could join me for the experiment." His broad, brilliant, charismatic smile encompassed them all, even Caryl. It was as if the Professor she'd seen in his office had never existed.

As if she really *had* imagined the whole thing.

The Professor plunged on with his speech, spinning the words around them all to make a dizzyingly fascinating net.

And Caryl knew, as she listened, that whatever else Professor DeLure was, he was irresistible.

Taking a deep breath, Caryl allowed herself to be swept along with the rest of the class.

"Okay," concluded Professor DeLure, and Caryl wasn't the only one who jumped, shocked at how quickly the time had gone. "Any questions?"

"I'm not sure I understand the assignment," said the cheerleader.

The Professor raised his eyebrow in what Caryl was already beginning to recognize as a characteristic response. His gaze swept the room and, somehow, Caryl was raising her hand.

"Ms. — Amberly, isn't it?"

Caryl nodded, her throat dry. "It's sort of like that poem by Carl Sandburg, in a way, isn't it? The one that describes the fog: 'The fog comes on little cat feet.' ''

"Exactly! Precisely," said the Professor. "Excellent, Ms. Amberly."

Unaware of the resentful looks sent her way, Caryl reveled in the praise as Professor De-Lure went on. "Observe. Use the eye of the scientist. Make scientific notes. Dispassionate. Clinical. Then take those notes and use the eye of the writer, the poet. Bring in passion. Put the two together. Bring me back a poem — and a page, one single, precise, accurate page of notes."

"But where are we going to find a dog or a cat to watch for an hour, on campus? You said we had to observe a dog or a cat . . ." persisted the cheerleader.

The clock chimed, signaling the end of the hour. The professor held up his finger. "Time," he said simply and walked out of the room.

Still caught in his spell, the class sat without moving for a moment longer. Then the cheerleader stood up. "Go, team, go," he said dryly, and the spell was broken.

Caryl gathered up her books, her head spinning, her cheeks still flushed with pleasure from Professor DeLure's praise. She didn't realize she had company until she'd started down the front steps of Griswold and a voice at her shoulder drawled, "So, little cat feet, where do you think you can find a cat or dog around here to observe for one hour?"

Caryl looked up and felt the warmth in her cheeks spread throughout her whole body.

Dare Winters was walking beside her.

"Cat?" she repeated stupidly, turning automatically in the direction of the student center.

"Or dog," answered Dare, a small smile on his face.

"The park," she heard herself say, as if it was the most obvious thing in the world. "Prospect Park. People walk their dogs there all the time. And there are special areas where the dogs can run and play off their leashes."

"Excellent," said Dare softly.

"Isn't it wonderful how some people know all about *dogs*." Perri had turned up, as usual. Just like a bad penny, thought Caryl. And as usual, she'd made Caryl seem like a silly child.

But surprisingly, Dare didn't seem to think so. " 'The more I see of people, the more I like my dog,' " he said easily. "I'm not sure who said that. Mark Twain, maybe?"

"I think Perri is more of a cat . . . person," Caryl couldn't resist saying.

Dare looked amused. Perri looked furious. She gave Caryl an evil look from narrow green eyes, then turned and flounced away.

"Bye, Perri," Caryl called after her.

"So you want to give me a guided tour of dog world in the park?" asked Dare. They reached the student center and he stopped and turned to face her.

Such blue, blue eyes . . .

"Me?" asked Caryl. "I mean, sure. Of course. No problem."

"Great," said Dare. "How about tomorrow afternoon, four o'clock? I'll meet you at the Pennsylvania Avenue entrance to the park."

"Great," said Caryl.

"Great," echoed Dare, teasing her a little. "Gotta make a class. See ya then."

"See ya," answered Caryl.

Incredible. Wonderful. Life really couldn't be better.

Caught up in her own thoughts, Caryl never even noticed the figure who'd emerged from the post office while she'd been standing and talking to Dare. She didn't see the scowl on the person's face or the rage in the person's eyes.

If she had, she might not have been so happy . . .

Chapter 6

Whistling as if she were calling a dog, Perri stepped in front of Caryl as she walked down the stairs to the post office the next morning.

"I didn't know cats could whistle," said Caryl. "Excuse me, please." She brushed past Perri and kept going. Why ruin a perfect day?

"You think you know so much, but you don't," Perri hissed after her. "Dare's only interested in you because it's a good way to make points with the teacher — little teacher's pet!"

Refusing to dignify Perri's words with an answer, Caryl kept walking. Perri was so insanely jealous, she thought. Just because Professor DeLure had said one nice thing to her.

And just because Dare hadn't fallen all over Perri like an average guy would have. Which just proved that Dare wasn't average.

And neither was Professor DeLure.

Still, Perri's words hurt.

But Caryl didn't look back.

She made herself concentrate instead on good things. Dare. How to shape her poem on what she'd see in the park. Even the mail. Maybe she would get a letter from a friend. Or one of those letters saying, "You have won a million dollars."

If I won a million dollars, she thought, I'd use some of it to have Perri . . . no . . . no.

She bent down, as usual, trying to peer into her mailbox. As usual, she couldn't see.

So why did she always try to look anyway? That would make an interesting scientific question, she thought wryly, twirling the combination. Maybe it's something Anna would like to do a study on.

The mailbox swung open and she reached inside. Her groping fingers closed around a slightly damp padded envelope. Probably a campus mailing of some kind, she thought, pulling it out.

But it wasn't.

Her name and box number were in big, childish print on the outside.

I guess I didn't win a million dollars, she thought, puzzled.

She pulled the tape off and opened the envelope. And froze.

Lying inside a folded sheet of notebook paper

was a small red fish with black markings. It was dead.

With a convulsive shriek, Caryl shook the fish and paper out of her hands.

"Ugh, ugh!" she cried, wiping her hand on her jeans.

"Caryl!"

"Anna! Oh my God!" Wordlessly, Caryl pointed.

Anna followed the direction of Caryl's finger and her eyes widened. Then, slowly, deliberately, she walked over and picked up the dead fish by the tail.

"Euuuw! How can you do that?"

"Where did this come from?" asked Anna.

"It was," Caryl shuddered, remembering the damp, clammy little fish body slithering out of the envelope into her hand, "it was in my mailbox. In an envelope. Inside that piece of paper."

Again Anna stooped and picked up the piece of paper Anna pointed out. She studied it for a moment, then read aloud softly, *"Roses are red/Violets are blue/Guess what I'm going/to do to you."*

"God," breathed Anna. "That's totally sick. Really ill."

"Yeah, no kidding."

Realizing that she was still clutching the envelope in her hand, Caryl turned it over and examined it.

Anna looked over her shoulder. "No return address, I guess," she said.

"No." Anna's unflappable response was having a calming affect on Caryl. At least she stiffled the urge to keep wiping her hands clean from the remembered feel of the dead fish. "What a sick joke," said Caryl.

"Joke? Do you think it's a joke?" Anna frowned.

"What else could it be?"

"I don't know. It's kind of scary."

Caryl studied the note for another minute. "Scary that someone could write so badly," she said, trying to sound unperturbed.

But she could tell Anna wasn't fooled. Regarding Caryl intently, Anna said, "You have any idea who it might be?"

"I don't know." Caryl suddenly flashed on Perri Biddle, the hissed words of hatred that Perri had thrown after her only a few minutes earlier. "Except maybe Perri."

"Perri?" Anna sounded surprised. "Why would Perri start doing something like this all of a sudden. I mean, I personally think Perri is a few chips shy of the cookie, but this kind of sick?"

"Who else could it be?" Caryl argued.

"Who else knew about your close encounter of the possibly weird kind with Professor DeLure? Besides me, I mean."

Caryl paused. Then she gasped. "Ben!"

Even as she was saying his name aloud, Caryl was pushing past Anna back toward the post office package window.

"Where are you going?" asked Anna.

Without answering, Caryl marched up to the package window. "Is Ben Cage here?"

The work-study student at the package window took one look at Caryl's white face and blazing eyes and nodded mutely.

"Could I speak to him please?"

With another quick nod, the student scurried away. A moment later, Ben emerged from the depths of the post office. He saw Caryl standing outside the package window and for a moment his face was expressionless. Then he broke into a wide grin.

"Hey, Caryl! D'ja come to play post office?"

"I'm *not* laughing Ben. This time, you've gone too far." Caryl held out the letter, noting as she did so that at least her hands had stopped shaking.

Ben took the paper uncertainly.

"Read it," ordered Caryl.

When he had finished, she pointed to the dead fish Anna was still holding in her hand.

"It came wrapped around that fish."

"What are you saying?" Ben's expression was bewildered. Then he turned a fiery red under his freckles. "Are you saying you think *I* sent this to you? Are you *crazy*?"

"No, Ben, I'm not. But I'm angry. Very angry."

"Well I am, too!"

Despite the rage that was consuming her, Caryl was startled by gentle Ben's ferociousness. She'd never seen him even betray impatience.

"I'm angry you'd think I'd do something like this. How could you? You think this is the way I treat people I care about?"

"Well if you didn't, who did? Who else besides you and Anna knew about that fish in Professor DeLure's office yesterday? Who else could have put this in my mailbox?"

Ben said, "One, I don't know who else knew. Except your precious professor. And two, anybody could have sent this through the campus mail. Anybody."

Caryl stared at Ben. He met her gaze levelly, his lips still thin with anger, but more hurt than anger in his eyes.

"You didn't do this?"

"No," said Ben.

Caryl knew he was telling the truth. "God, Ben, I'm sorry."

For a moment, a grim, strange Ben looked back at her. Then his face softened. "It's okay, Caryl. It's pretty freaky."

"I'm so sorry," said Caryl again, laying her hand on his arm. He put his own hand over hers and smiled a little and she was relieved to see the hurt expression leaving his face.

Then Anna interrupted, practical as always. "So if you didn't send it, Ben, who did?"

The thought gnawed at Caryl. Who, who, who, she wondered, the words drumming out in time to her footsteps.

Perri. It had to be Perri. But Anna was so sure it wasn't that Caryl found herself shaken in her belief.

But then who?

It wasn't until she caught sight of Dare at the entrance to Prospect Park that the question stopped repeating itself in her head.

She smiled at him, and the question and fear fled and she fell into step beside him easily. *As if I'd been doing this forever*, she thought. Despite the erratic pounding of her heart brought on by just seeing Dare, Caryl felt comfortable next to him.

Soon they'd staked out a small hill above a

dog play area and settled down to watch and make notes.

"I'm going with that bull terrier," said Dare almost immediately. "I like the way she stands her ground."

Caryl laughed. "She's cute. I'm going for the greyhound, though. He's gorgeous. . . . do you think the owners look like their dogs?"

"Hmm. Some do . . . But do you think they looked like their dogs before they got their dogs — or after? Like, did that guy with the red hair dye his hair before he got his Irish setter or vice versa?"

Caryl narrowed her eyes. "His hair *is* dyed!" she exclaimed in amazement.

"You thought that color was for real?" asked Dare.

She met Dare's eyes and both burst into laughter. Soon, as they made notes and watched the dogs and their people, Caryl found herself telling Dare about the small midwestern town she'd come from, and what it was like being the oldest child in the family. Dare, it turned out, was too.

"Oldest of the litter," he said, shaking his head. "It's a tough job. You have to get in a *lot* of trouble to soften the parental units up for your little brothers and sisters."

"Not me," said Caryl, assuming an angelic expression. "I was always good and perfect, so they'd have to live up to my high standards."

"Yeah, right," Dare answered. Then he added more softly, "How good are you?"

She looked up and met his eyes and held them for a long moment. Then she said, "Maybe you'll find out."

I can't believe I said that, she thought. But Dare didn't seem to mind. He looked at her for another long moment, then grinned. "I think I'd like that," he said.

Flipping his notebook shut, he jumped to his feet. "We've done our hour."

Caryl realized with surprise that it was true. She reached up to the hand Dare stretched out to her and let herself be pulled to her feet. He kept her hand in his as they walked out of the park.

Holding Dare's hand was much more interesting than holding Ben's hand. Caryl couldn't believe how easy it was to be with Dare. To talk to him.

So easy that, before she knew it, as they were leaving the park, she found herself confiding in him about the note, the dead fish, and the encounter with Professor DeLure.

He stopped. "You're kidding," he said.

She shook her head. "And I can't think who, or why. I've never had any enemies before. Not any enemies like this."

"Whoever did this sounds like a pretty sick puppy, if you'll pardon the expression."

"Yeah." Caryl sighed. "Well, I guess it kind of goes with Salem. I mean we do have a dorm called Nightmare Hall, after all."

"Yeah — Nightmare Hall, where the girl died. Well, listen, Caryl, I don't know who your enemy might be, but will you count me as a friend? In fact, let's make plans for this weekend and we'll talk about it."

Caryl met Dare's eyes. The expression in them made her feel dizzy.

But when Dare's lips touched hers, she knew she wasn't dizzy. It was the whole world spinning around in her head.

"Hi, girls and boys!"

Still feeling as if she were on a carnival ride, Caryl stepped confusedly back.

Perri was bearing down on them.

Caryl looked up at Dare. A little smile quirked his mouth.

Caryl smiled back and turned. "Hi Perri," she gushed. "What a nice surprise. I was just leaving."

"See ya," she said to Dare and for the second

time that day she turned her back on Perri Biddle and walked away.

"See you, friend," said Dare after her, and hearing that, Caryl knew that nothing Perri or anyone could do would change the way she felt.

Chapter 7

The final bell rang.

Caryl jumped.

She'd been so totally caught up in the Professor's performance that she had, as usual, been unaware of the passing of time.

Professor DeLure stopped in mid-sentence. "Well," he said. "An excellent class." His eyes roamed the room and settled on Caryl. "Excellent," he repeated.

And Caryl felt that somehow, he meant what he said exclusively for her.

"Nicholas, if you would be so kind as to return everyone's most recent assignments to them . . ." The Professor strode from the room and Nicholas France, who'd been sitting in the back of the class, got up.

He stopped for a moment at Caryl's desk and regarded her speculatively as he handed her her most recent poem. Across the top, written in red ink in the Professor's scrawling, distinctive hand, the word *Excellent* blazed.

"Nice work," said Nicholas. "So — what do you think of Professor DeLure?"

For a moment, Caryl was tempted to try to be sophisticated, to act as if the word *Excellent* from Professor DeLure were all in a day's homework. But the still seriousness of Nicholas's expression stopped her.

"He's incredible," she said at last. "The best teacher I've ever had."

As if Caryl had passed some test, Nicholas's face broke into an unexpectedly warm smile. "Yeah. But it's not often he gets students like you, who know how to appreciate him. I mean really appreciate him. Students who can measure up."

Surprised and pleased, Caryl returned Nicholas's smile. "Thank you," she said.

"Don't thank me for being yourself," said Nicholas, and moved down the row of desks to finish handing out the papers.

Flushed with the Professor's praise and Nicholas's words, Caryl drifted dreamily out into the hall, holding the paper in her hand.

"Ms. Amberly."

She stopped and looked up. Professor DeLure was standing at the foot of the stairs, obviously on his way up to his office.

"Oh! Professor DeLure! Uh, thank you for
. . ." Caught off guard, she lost the thread of
her sentence and settled for holding up the paper in her hand.

"You don't thank your teacher for something
you've earned. Rather, the teacher thanks the
student."

"I don't know about that." Caryl swallowed
hard. "I mean, I've had good teachers before,
but you're, you know, you're the best."

The Professor's sternly expressionless face
relaxed into the smallest of smiles. "I thank
you." The Professor raised his voice slightly,
addressing a woman who had just come down
the hall. "Professor Perez. This is the student
I was telling you about — Caryl Amberly. Ms.
Amberly, this is the chairwoman of the science
department, as you may know."

A silver-haired woman with piercing eyes
had paused at the Professor's words and now
turned to smile at Caryl. "Ah. Professor
DeLure has spoken highly of you on more than
one occasion, Ms. Amberly. He says you have
a rare talent. You are not, unfortunately, a
science major, I take it?"

"English," confessed Caryl.

"Too bad. You might reconsider — possibly
even a double major. The ability to combine
scientific thought and clarity of expression is

all *too* rare, as Professor DeLure is discovering."

Embarrassed, Caryl said, "Well, uh . . ."

"Plenty of time to be thinking about that, though, since you're a first-year student. I'm pleased to have met you. Professor." The chairwoman nodded and walked briskly up the stairs.

"Professor, I'm glad I caught up with you." Nicholas came up beside Caryl, and gave her a broad smile and the smallest of winks.

"I will see you later, Ms. Amberly," said the Professor softly, looking into Caryl's eyes. Then he turned and fell into step beside Nicholas saying, "Yes, Nicholas, what is it?"

Caryl walked to her next class in a daze. How could she ever have been afraid of Professor DeLure? How could anyone ever think he was hard or unfair?

He was wonderful. Life was wonderful. She'd never been so happy.

"How was the great Professor DeLure for you today?" said Anna. She dumped a cup of detergent into her laundry and thumped the washer door shut. She and Caryl were in the Quad basement.

Caryl rolled her eyes. She hadn't told Anna about what the Professor had said to her earlier in the day. She hadn't told anyone. She wanted to keep the memory for herself, treasure it. "Rare talent" he had said. She smiled, recalling the words.

"Well, he was a gorilla, an absolute animal in Intro Biology today. I've gotta tell you, something about the way he was waving that specimen knife around was making me dead nervous . . ."

"Puh-leeze," said Caryl. "Give it up, Anna."

Anna cocked her head. Then she said, softly, "Caryl?"

"What?"

"Don't you have a date with Ben tonight?"

"Geez, I'd almost forgotten!" Caryl looked at her watch. "I'd better hurry."

"Poor Ben," said Anna. "It's hard for him to compete with poetry professors, I guess."

"Anna! Besides, I don't think of the Professor *that* way. He's a — a mentor."

Anna gave Caryl a small, sly smile. "Do you think of Dare Winters *that* way?"

Caryl couldn't help herself. She could feel herself begin to blush. "That," she assured Anna, trying to maintain her dignity, "is an entirely different story. Good-*bye!*"

Ben was waiting for her in the dorm lobby when she hurried downstairs a short while later, breathless but almost exactly on time.

"Ben," she said, and the nagging sense of guilt she'd been feeling about him made her give him an extra-high-wattage smile.

Ben looked pleased. He leaned over and kissed her lightly on the cheek.

"Your turn," he said, taking her arm as they went out.

"My turn?"

"Don't you remember — to choose the movie."

"Oh." She laughed. "But if I choose it, I can't complain about it, right?"

"Yeah, well, it does sorta work that way."

"Then you choose it. Even if it *is* a scary one."

Ben looked even more pleased. How simple he was, how easy to make happy. Why couldn't she be more interested in someone like Ben? Good, easygoing Ben. Not that Dare Winters didn't seem easygoing. But he didn't feel that way. In fact, Dare felt distinctly, deliciously dangerous . . .

"The first *Halloween* is playing at the Screening Room," suggested Ben hopefully.

Shaking the thought of Dare from her mind, Caryl said, "Let's go!"

Still feeling guilty about accusing Ben of trying to scare her — and maybe also about thinking of Dare in spite of all she could do not to — Caryl held Ben's hand tightly all through the movie and pretended to be more frightened than she was in the scary parts. Afterwards, as they started toward the parking lot where Ben kept his beat-up old car, Caryl realized it had been a mistake.

When they got into the car, instead of turning on the motor, Ben reached over and pulled Caryl toward him. "Caryl," he said, his voice husky.

She turned her head slightly and Ben's kiss touched her cheek. "Ben," she began.

He didn't seem to hear her.

"Caryl," he said. "I love you so much. I've been wanting to tell you."

"*Love?* Ben. . . ."

He went on, ignoring her. "The moment I saw you in the post office that first week of school, I knew you were the only one for me. That I'd been waiting for you all my life. Oh, Caryl." His arms tightened around her. He kissed her hard, oblivious to her resistance.

But then she managed to pull away. She put her hand up against Ben's chest. "Ben, please. I can't. It's not . . . it's not right."

Ben leaned back abruptly, staring at her through the shadowy dark. "What?"

"I'm sorry if I gave you the impression that

this was more serious than it was. I like you a lot, I really do, Ben. But I don't, I can't love you. Not like that."

"What are you saying?"

"I hope we can be friends, Ben."

Ben burst out, "Friends! It's someone else, isn't it, Caryl? Who? Who is it?

"No one! I'm not ready to be serious about anyone yet."

To Caryl's amazement, Ben suddenly shouted, "Tell me the truth! It's that Winters guy, isn't it? Isn't it!"

For an astonished moment, Caryl could only stare at Ben. How did he know about Dare? She'd only been to the park with Dare and walked with him after class. They hadn't even had a real date yet. Not until the weekend.

How could Ben know anything about Dare?

She found her voice at last. "What are you talking about?"

Ben's face, so open, so friendly, so kind, had turned into the face of a stranger. His eyes were hard, his mouth thin. "I know what I know. You can't do that to me, Caryl. You can't cheat on me like that."

His voice was low and menacing. He moved toward her and grabbed her arm, his grip hard and painful.

"Let go of me!" Caryl demanded.

In answer, Ben pulled her toward him again. "You're mine," he said. "Mine."

With a desperate effort, Caryl jerked free. She lunged across the seat and threw the door of the car open and tumbled out.

"Caryl! Wait!"

She didn't stop or answer. She heard Ben turn on the motor of his car. And she began to run as hard as she could across the parking lot, away from Ben, to somewhere, anywhere safe.

Chapter 8

The car roared out of the parking lot, pinning Caryl with its lights. Desperately, she leaped to one side out of their beams and plunged down an alley.

The tires screamed as Ben braked. She ran on, faster, faster.

Then the car was behind her.

No matter how fast she ran, she could never outrun it.

What was Ben going to do?

Ahead a fence loomed.

She was trapped. She slowed. The car behind her kept coming as fast as before.

Was he going to kill her?

She didn't wait to find out. With one last desperate effort, she flung herself at it, scrabbling up the chain links.

The car stopped. The door opened.

A hand grabbed her foot.

"No," she gasped, "No!" She kicked backwards and felt her foot crunch against flesh and bone.

Ben gave a strangled howl.

She swung over the fence and landed on all fours on the ground. She was in someone's backyard. A dog began to bark from inside the house. The lights came on.

Unthinking, unheeding, Caryl blundered across the yard. Through the light coming from a window she saw a gate and, even as she saw it, she was coming up to it, opening it, running through.

"Caryl!" shouted Ben. "Caryllll!"

She kept running.

She didn't know how long she ran. Her jeans were ripped. Her scraped hands were on fire. She couldn't breathe.

She slowed.

No one was behind her. She had escaped.

An ominous crack of thunder split the sky and she looked up.

"Great," she muttered.

She bent over to put her hands gingerly on her knees, trying to catch her breath.

Lightning crackled, followed almost immediately by another crash of thunder.

"Just great," she gasped, and straightening

up, began to walk shakily toward what looked like a busy street ahead.

The thunder and lightning were practically simultaneous this time, followed by the first bullets of rain.

Caryl raised her arm to wipe the sweat and water from her face and peered through the beginnings of the storm. She was standing at the foot of a driveway leading up to a large old house. With one last burst of energy, she stumbled up the steps just as a sheet of rain fell from the sky.

The claps of thunder made the porch rock. The lightning was blinding. And the rain was so ferocious that the porch of the big old house offered hardly any shelter at all.

Wet, shivering, exhausted, she raised her hand to knock at the door, to ask for some help.

"Be home," she whispered. "Somebody please be home."

It seemed impossible that anyone could hear her knock through the noise of the storm. But she had scarcely rapped on the door before it swung open.

They must have seen me, thought Caryl. She pasted a smile on her face, hoping she didn't look as wild and bedraggled as she felt.

But no one was there.

"Hello?" called Caryl.

No answer.

She stepped hesitantly into the dim hall. The house was dark.

"Hello," she called again.

"Hello." The voice that answered was a breath, a whisper, without any inflection to it at all.

Caryl jumped. As if she had materialized out of the darkness, a slim girl with long blonde hair stood at Caryl's elbow.

"Oh! Oh, you startled me. The door was open. I got caught in the storm and was wondering if maybe I could borrow a towel or something."

"Wait here," said the girl in the same expressionless tone, and was gone as suddenly as she had appeared.

Caryl blinked. How had she done that?

"I guess the storm must have gotten your electricity," she said loudly, rubbing her arms to keep them warm as a cold shiver ran over her.

No one answered. Another flash of lightning showed the hall in stark relief. Empty. Caryl backed up a step and glanced over her shoulder. The storm was still at fever pitch.

"Here." The word was in Caryl's ear. She spun around to see the girl holding out a towel at arm's length. When Caryl reached for the towel the girl let it go, almost as if she were afraid of Caryl touching her.

"Thanks," said Caryl, catching the towel gratefully. She rubbed her wet hair and blotted the worst of the water out of her clothes. But it didn't help that much. It was so *cold*. Why hadn't she worn a jacket that evening?

"I guess that'll take care of me until I can get home," said Caryl, handing the towel back to the girl.

The girl stepped away and motioned with one pale white hand. "Put it on the table. There."

"Oh. Okay."

Weird, thought Caryl, folding the towel and laying it on the table. Does she think she's going to catch something from me, or what?

Another bolt of lightning illuminated the hall, blotting the pale figure of the girl from Caryl's vision in the blinding flash. She blinked, trying to focus.

The thunder rumbled, much more softly and farther away and as abruptly as it had begun, the freak thunderstorm began to slack off.

"I guess I'd better get back to Salem," said Caryl. "I'm a student there. My name's Caryl."

"I'm Giselle. You can catch a bus on the corner," the girl intoned, as if she were reciting an almost forgotten lesson. She raised her hand stiffly and pointed.

"Wow, that's great . . . the storm came up so fast, I kinda got turned around."

The girl stood motionless, her long hair stirring slightly in the chill air.

gotta   Feeling uneasy, Caryl smiled politely. "Well, gotta go. Thanks again."

Liselle didn't answer.

Caryl turned and pulled the door open.

The rain had almost completely stopped.

With a feeling of relief, Caryl walked out into the wet, cool air. She had to fight herself not to run down the steps.

No doubt about it. The whole night was getting to her.

"*Night of the Living Dead*," muttered Caryl. "Yeah, right."

At the foot of the front walk she stopped and frowned. The lights up and down the road were all shining brightly. Had they been able to get the electricity back on that fast?

Caryl turned. The house behind her was dark. And silhouetted against the dark mouth of the open door, stood the still, pale figure of Giselle.

Suddenly the girl raised her hand. Before Caryl's astonished, horrified gaze, she began to fade, to bleed from white into terrifying darkness. "Carylll," she called in a keen, sad voice, "Caryllll. Beware the one who hides what he is. Beware the one who waits. . . . Beware the one who is clothed in death. . . . Beware. . . . Death . . . beware. . . ."

On the last word, Giselle vanished completely.

Caryl fell back and stumbled against something. She looked down. It was a Salem U housing sign. By the reflection of the streetlight, Caryl read in neat gothic lettering the words:

Nightingale Hall.

Chapter 9

Steamy heat rose from the water boiling down into the bathtub. Bubbles foamed and the heavy scent of bubble bath rose on the steam. Caryl had the long, gleaming white and chrome dorm bathroom to herself.

She wasn't sure whether she was glad or sorry. When she had gotten back to the Quad, her clothes still damp from her run through the rain, her mouth still dry from her encounter with Giselle, she'd been relieved her roommate wasn't home to ask questions. It had been hard enough to pass the resident advisor on duty at the front desk of the Quad, who'd fixed Caryl with a piercing eye and said, "Are you in some sort of trouble? Is something wrong?"

"I got caught in the rain. Just cold," Caryl had assured her. And she had nodded obediently when the RA had told her to get out of her wet clothes and into a hot bath. It was comforting, somehow, to be treated like a child for a moment.

But she wasn't a child.

She had to face what was going on.

Whatever it was.

With a deep sigh, she switched off the water, and slid into the bath beneath the bubbles until her chin was resting on them.

Think, she told herself. You have to think.

What is happening to you? What is going on here?

Some weirdo just warned you your life was in danger. Some weirdo in a haunted house.

Unless someone was playing a joke on her.

A long, elaborate, mean joke. A joke that started with threatening notes and a dead fish in her mailbox and had moved on to spooky occurrences in an allegedly haunted house.

No. That last had been a coincidence. No way anyone could have known Caryl would end up there tonight. What had happened at Nightingale Hall was an isolated incident. Everyone said that house was a real creepshow. The girl who'd answered the door was probably some nerdy study rat Caryl had gotten out of bed. That was it.

But who had sent the poem and put the dead fish in her mailbox?

Perri? The bad poetry was certainly Perri's

style. But how had she known about the Siamese fighting fish? Caryl hadn't told anyone about that.

Except Anna and Ben. It was Anna who'd known about the fish, what kind they were. Trust Anna to know some obscure detail like that.

Maybe it had been Ben. After tonight, Caryl could believe that of him. After tonight, she could believe anything of Ben.

Except that it didn't quite fit. If he loved her, he wouldn't do a sick thing like that.

Had Anna told Perri? Caryl couldn't believe she had. Anna disliked Perri almost as much as Caryl — and every other girl in the first-year class at Salem — did.

Could Perri have followed Caryl that first night when she'd gone over to visit the Professor? That made a sort of odd sense, thought Caryl, when you considered that Perri had obviously followed Caryl and Dare to the park.

Hmmm.

Caryl reached up with her foot and turned on more hot water. Trying to think things through, to reason them out, was relaxing her, in a way, almost as much as the hot water was. She made a face. Maybe that's why Anna always seemed so calm. Maybe there was a lot more to be said for a rational, scientific turn of mind than Caryl had thought.

So maybe it could have been Perri. Maybe — maybe Ben had told Perri what had happened.

He didn't know how Perri and Caryl felt about each other. Maybe Perri had pried the information out of Ben. Knowing Perri, Caryl knew it would have been second nature to her.

Maybe it was something Ben had just mentioned to Perri in passing.

Or maybe it was a conspiracy.

Sure, Caryl, she mocked herself. And maybe you really are going crazy.

The thought sobered her. She was sure — well, almost sure — that she had imagined the intensity, the strangeness of her first meeting with Professor DeLure. Every class since then, every encounter had been so wonderful.

And maybe she had imagined the strangeness of her encounter with the girl at Nightmare Hall.

But she hadn't imagined the words. She was sure of that. Beware.

Death.

The water was beginning to grow cold. Reluctantly Caryl opened the drain and got out of the bathtub. The face that stared back at her from the mirror now wasn't as pale and wild as it had been.

But for a moment, just a moment, it seemed like the face of a stranger. The face of a girl that someone hated. That someone wanted to scare. To hurt.

To kill.

That isn't me, she thought. I've never had any real enemies. Never.

Only friends.

But now all that had changed.

And Caryl realized what it was she saw in her face now.

Fear. The fear of the hunted.

"Caryl, it's for you." Caryl's roommate handed her the phone and ducked out of the room, headed for class.

"Hello?"

"Hello," a husky voice breathed, and for one awful moment, Caryl's heart went into triple overdrive. For one awful moment, she thought the voice was Ben's.

Or worse . . . the soft, haunting voice of Giselle . . .

"Who — who is it?" she croaked.

"How quickly I'm forgotten," the voice mourned. "It's Dare Winters. We met in Professor Maximillian DeLure's class. Shared a very nice homework assignment. I thought we were — friends. But I guess being the class star has made you forget those who knew you when."

"I'm *not* the class star!" Caryl almost snapped. Get a grip, she told herself. She paused, then said, "I mean, it's nice of you to say and all, Dare, but it's just not true."

"Whatever the lady says," Dare answered easily. "As long as she says yes, we're still going out this weekend."

"Yes. The lady says yes, yes, yes," said Caryl, her annoyance forgotten.

"There's a reading — that poet guy the Professor was talking about, remember? Want to go to that?"

"Do you?" asked Caryl.

"Sure, why not? It'll be a new experience."

Caryl laughed, remembering how difficult it had been to persuade Ben to try *anything* new. "Let's try it then. I've never done anything like that either."

"Great," said Dare. "It's at eight so I'll come by for you a little after seven. And maybe afterwards, we can try out some other things we haven't done."

"Pizza?" Caryl teased. "You do mean going out for pizza, don't you?"

Dare laughed softly. "See you tomorrow night," he said.

Still smiling, Caryl hung up the phone.

Friends, she thought. Being friends with Dare was going to give a whole new meaning to the word.

The high from Dare's phone call lasted through the rest of the day. Made her a little less jumpy about the possibility of running into Ben. Made her forget, a little, about everything that had been happening.

Until that night, when she was almost asleep. And Dare's words came back to her. *Class star*.

It was just an innocent phrase, she thought. Dare didn't mean anything by it.

I can trust Dare, she thought. I know I can. If I can't trust him, who can I trust?

Chapter 10

"Strange," said Dare, offering Caryl a cup of soda. "That poet guy was definitely weird. But I guess poets are like that." They were at the Kennels, an off-campus dorm for some of the Salem guys. Caryl had never been to a party there before, and when Dare suggested they stop there after the reading it had seemed like just the right antidote to the week she'd been having.

"Weird?" asked Caryl, hiding a smile.

"Yeah. But it was kinda interesting, too. I mean, some of that stuff was amazing. I don't see how he thought of it."

"Me either." Caryl sighed. "I wish I did."

"Hey, you do *excellent*ly well," said Dare. "No complaints from Professor DeLure, right?" Before Caryl could demur, Dare leaned over and tapped her pack. "You took notes, too. Pretty impressive. I mean, I know the Prof suggested we go to this and all, but still. . . ."

Embarrassed, remembering how she'd been teased before by others for "taking notes" in the notebook she always carried with her, Caryl laughed and shrugged.

But Dare wasn't making fun of her. "Seriously," he said. "You're dedicated. That's impressive. To care more about what you think, about what feels right for you, than what others try to tell you, that's important."

Caryl felt herself blushing and was glad that the party was reasonably dark.

"We can leave anytime," he said now, nodding toward the people dancing across the room from where they sat. "But I'd like to dance a little first. What about you?"

In answer, Caryl stashed her pack under the sofa, put down the soda, and let Dare pull her to her feet. As they got to the floor, the music downshifted abruptly into a slow dance.

Without a pause, Dare pulled Caryl into his arms.

She leaned against him and for the first time all week felt safe. Warm.

And possibly as if she were falling in love.

Is this what it's like? she wondered. Not bad. Not bad at all. . . .

"I didn't know you two knew each other so well. Wasn't your little friend Ben enough for you, Caryl? I thought I saw him here earlier. But maybe I was mistaken."

As Dare's arms tightened around her, Caryl knew without opening her eyes that it was Perri. Again. How did she *do* that?

"I guess Dare didn't tell you what good friends he and I are, did he, Caryl?" Perri's voice went on.

Caryl lifted her head from Dare's shoulder and met Perri's eyes. What she saw there almost made her flinch away. Perri's eyes, in contrast to the brilliant smile on her face, were dark pits of rage.

"It didn't seem important, Perri," Dare answered before Caryl could speak. "It's ancient history. Over. Done with. Let it go."

The blaze in Perri's eyes, impossibly, increased. "Really?" she purred. She stepped close to the two of them, too close.

Caryl forced herself not to shrink away. To meet Perri's blood-hungry glare.

"Just remember this, little teacher's pet," Perri went on, her eyes never leaving Caryl's face. "History repeats itself. Even ancient history. . . ."

Perri turned on her heel and was gone.

* * *

"So how was it?"

Caryl smiled mysteriously. She'd just gotten back from her date with Dare to find a note from Anna stuck in the door, threatening her with a "fate worse then death if you don't come and tell me *everything — tonight!*"

Stopping only long enough to drop her pack on the bed and to go downstairs and grab a couple of sodas from the vending machines in the basement, Caryl had obeyed Anna's summons. Now they were propped against the wall in the hall outside Anna's door, since Anna's roommate was already asleep.

"Caryl! Tell me!" demanded Anna.

"It was . . . great. Even running into Perri at the Kennels didn't ruin the night. In fact, it made the end of the evening . . . extra nice."

"The Kennels?" Anna sounded surprised. "You didn't say you were at that party!"

"Yeah. Wait a minute, how did you know about it?"

Anna looked guiltily away, a faint, telltale blush turning the tips of her ears red.

"Anna, tell me," Caryl demanded in turn.

"Well, you know I had that blind date?"

"And?"

"It was the usual blind date disaster. But he

did take me to the party at the Kennels."

"Anna! You were there? Why didn't I see you?"

"We must have left before you got there. Anyway it wasn't a complete loss because . . ."

"Because why?" prompted Caryl.

"Because Nicholas was there."

"Nicholas?" For a moment, Caryl was at a loss.

"Nicholas France. Professor DeLure's grad student assistant. Caryl! How could you forget him?"

Easily, Caryl almost said. But she didn't. Instead, she said, "Oh *that* Nicholas. I didn't see him there, either."

"I guess he left early. He works really hard, you know. Anyway, enough about me and Nicholas."

"You and Nicholas?" teased Caryl.

"Tell me what happened with you and Dare," Anna went on, her composure restored.

"Don't think you're getting off that easy, Anna. But okay, me and Dare. What can I say? It was wonderful."

The two girls grinned at each other, and by mutual consent slid a little lower against the hall wall, getting comfortable for a good, long, late-night talk.

I'm so lucky, thought Caryl, *to have Anna*

for my best friend. I don't know what I'd do without her.

Dare and Anna. Friends. Different kinds of friends, but friends who'll stick by me no matter what. Through thick and thin.

I guess that's what friends are for.

Chapter 11

"Ms. Amberly."

"Professor DeLure?"

"Do you have a moment?"

Caryl looked at Dare, who glanced at the Professor and then back at Caryl. An ironic little smile curled his lips, but his voice was bland as he said to Caryl, "I'll catch you later."

Caryl nodded gratefully and turned her attention to Professor DeLure.

The Professor's gaze followed Dare as he left, then returned to Caryl. His own smile was, perhaps, even more ironic than Dare's had been — ironic and almost bitter. Caryl braced herself for the Professor's comment, but he merely lifted the eyebrow above his eyepatch.

To her dismay, Caryl heard herself stammer, "D-Dare and I are friends. I mean . . ."

"You owe me no explanation of your personal life, Ms. Amberly." His voice hardened and his eye grew dark and stormy. "Indeed, I have no say in anyone's life. That time has passed."

He paused, then went on, less coldly, "I merely wanted to ask you if you had a moment now to discuss your most recent assignment. I was impressed by some of your observations."

The odd, fearful constricting of her heart that Caryl had experienced when she'd thought the Professor was somehow displeased with her was replaced by a sheer rush of pleasure.

"Of course," she said. They'd reached the stairs. The Professor nodded and they started up toward the fourth floor and his office.

Did he remember their first meeting, wondered Caryl.

Or, for that matter, do I? Once again, as often happened in her encounters with Professor DeLure, she had a sensation of unreality, as if she and he were in a play.

Part of it, at least, was because of his courtly, almost old-fashioned manners, when he chose to exercise them, and his measured, deliberate way of speaking. Part of it, too, was his charm, so obviously easy for him to turn off and on. That, too, was something an actor could do.

Reaching the top of the stairs, Caryl realized that they had been walking in silence the whole way. She began to cast around desperately in her mind for something to say, but was saved by the appearance of Nicholas, popping up seemingly out of nowhere.

"Professor!"

"Nicholas." The Professor's voice, in marked contrast to Nicholas's enthusiasm, was measured and cold again.

"That problem I've been having with my thesis . . . I've almost got a handle on it. I was wondering if you could go over it with me."

"Certainly." The Professor kept walking and Nicholas fell into step on the other side of him.

"It's going to involve repeating some of the experiments, I'm afraid."

"Never be afraid to repeat something until you get it right," returned the Professor. He looked over at Caryl and his voice warmed perceptibly. "As true in poetry as in science, wouldn't you agree, Ms. Amberly?"

Nicholas couldn't help but notice the change in the Professor's tone, and he looked taken aback. But he persisted, saying as they stopped in front of the Professor's office door, "No. I understand that. Naturally."

"Naturally," murmured the Professor, sounding almost disdainful. He opened the door and sketched a small bow to Caryl. "Ms. Amberly."

Caryl walked ahead of the Professor and

Nicholas into the office. But when Nicholas tried to follow, the Professor held up his hand.

"I'm sure that discovering the precise nature of the difficulty in your thesis will prove fascinating, Nicholas. But not at the moment."

"But — " began Nicholas.

"We'll talk later." The Professor began to shut the door.

"Right, Professor," Nicholas said.

The door closed.

Caryl stood uncertainly in the middle of the room. It was just as she remembered it. Slowly, she forced herself to look at the aquarium behind the Professor's desk.

The Siamese fighting fish was still there, a motionless, blood-red outline hovering in the water.

Caryl looked away quickly.

What had she expected?

Nervously, she cleared her throat.

But the brusque man who had dismissed Nicholas was gone. Professor DeLure smiled at her and indicated the worn leather chair across from his desk. "Make yourself at home."

He sat in his own chair behind the desk and settled back, making a tent of his fingers.

"Ms. Amberly," he began.

"Caryl," Caryl blurted out. "You can call me Caryl."

The Professor paused, then smiled with genuine warmth. "Outside of class, I will certainly do so, then. Thank you. Caryl.

"Now, where were we? Ah, yes. Your most recent assignment. I was interested in the way you used rhythm patterns to approximate the sounds you described in your observation paper . . ."

How was I ever afraid of Professor DeLure, thought Caryl happily. *You just have to get to know him, that's all.*

The rest of the afternoon flew by, until the Professor reached up to turn on his desk lamp, looked at his watch, and exclaimed, "The time! I must go. And you have your own life to get on with. Caryl. No?"

Caryl realized the Professor was referring to Dare. But this time she didn't feel uncomfortable at all. She smiled back at Professor DeLure and stood up without answering.

"I'll walk you back to your dorm, or to the student center, if you're headed in that direction," said the Professor.

"You don't need to do that," Caryl told him.

"Ah, well. It will be my pleasure." He waved his hand, cutting off any argument, and Caryl soon found herself walking across the Salem campus toward the dorm with Professor DeLure. It was dark out, and they passed beneath the succession of globe lights that marked the campus paths as if they were moving in and out of spotlights on some vast, leafy stage. Many of the people who passed noticed Caryl, noticed the Professor. He was rarely seen in the company of anyone, and Caryl felt a certain pride in being seen with him, a pride made stronger by the fact that some of the glances directed her way were almost certainly awed, and a little envious.

When they reached the dorm, the Professor again executed one of his characteristic little half-bows.

"Thank you," said Caryl. "Thank you for all your help."

The Professor looked down at her and for a moment his expression was remote, sad. Then he said, "Not at all, Caryl. You have helped me, too. More than you can know."

Then he was gone.

Caryl stood for a moment, watching him disappear into the early evening dark.

Then she turned.

And stopped.

Someone was watching her. She could feel it. Feel it like the force of a blow against her skin.

Stop it, she told herself. Of course someone is watching you. You've just been seen in the company of Professor DeLure. You're standing in front of the entrance to an enormous first-year women's dorm. And there are zillions of windows looking out in this direction.

It would be amazing if you weren't being watched.

But the feeling persisted. The feeling of unease. The feeling that whoever was watching her wasn't merely doing so out of idle interest.

Against her will, she found herself hurrying into the dorm, into the safety and light and warmth.

The Quad Caf was deserted at this hour of the evening, Caryl noted with relief. After leaving Professor DeLure, she'd gone up to her room, mentally rolling up her sleeves for a long evening of work on her assignments — most specifically, her assignment for the Professor's class. But the room had felt claustrophobic. She'd thought for a moment about trying to find a room in the rabbit warren of rooms and halls that ran beneath the Quad called the Dungeon, but had rejected that idea, too. If her room, with its large windows looking out over campus, felt claustrophobic, the windowless, airless Dungeon was going to feel even worse.

Besides, she wanted privacy, not absolute

isolation. And there was something about the Quad basement that gave her the creeps. It was aptly dubbed the Dungeon, she thought.

So she'd opted for the small cafeteria at one corner of the Quad, next to the entrance. The coffee was, if anything, worse than the coffee at the student center caf, and most of the first-year women went to the student center except when they were crunching for tests or finals — which suited Caryl fine. Anyone in the Quad Caf would be totally focused on her own worries, and not into conversation.

Caryl bought a cup of coffee, laced it liberally with milk and sugar and carried it to a table in the corner. She hesitated for a moment, remembering the sensation of being watched earlier, then shook her head at her own imagination. If anybody was watching her now, they were lurking in the shrubbery inside the four buildings that formed the Quadrangle. Hardly likely.

She sat down and took a sip of coffee, added more sugar from the container on the table, then pulled her pack toward her. Her notebook tumbled out. Realizing that she hadn't looked in it or made any notes since the night of her poetry-reading date with Dare, Caryl smiled. So much had happened since then. She had a lot to write about.

With a glow of satisfaction at her good intentions, Caryl flipped the book open and riffled the pages.

And stopped, clutching one page so hard it tore beneath her suddenly nerveless fingers.

In slashing, exaggerated black letters, scrawled across the final pages of her notes, malignant words stared evilly back at her:

Star light, Star bright,
She's the teacher's pet tonight.
But when the sun begins to rise
Teacher's pet is going to die.

Chapter 12

"I don't believe it!" Anna gasped. "Caryl, when did this happen?"

"I don't know, I don't know!" Caryl almost wailed.

It had taken several minutes for the shock of the glaring, threatening words to sink in. Then Caryl had leaped to her feet, overturning her chair in which she was sitting. Heedless of the stares and whispers that followed her out of the Quad Caf, she had run blindly out, making her way almost by instinct to Anna's room. Fortunately, Anna had been there, her head bent above an Intro Psych book.

Anna closed Caryl's notebook, then opened it again, as if she hoped that closing it would make the words go away. But they were still there.

"Oh, God," said Anna. "This is serious. It's getting totally out of hand. Caryl, you've got to do something. Go to the campus police."

Caryl hesitated, then shook her head. "No. What can they do?"

"Then what are you going to do? Just wait until this, this joker, actually acts on one of his threats?"

Seeing the normally calm Anna so upset wasn't helping Caryl. She took a deep breath. "Let me think."

Anna waited, then said impatiently, "You think you can figure this out yourself. Okay. When did you last write in your notebook?" She fixed Caryl with an intent look, as if she could will the answer from her.

"The night of my date with Dare. I took it along to make notes at the poetry reading."

"Then what happened?"

Caryl said slowly, "I put it back in my pack. Dare and I talked a little about it at the party. I didn't tell him it was a journal, too. I mean, that I had my — private — thoughts in there. He thinks I'm just keeping notes for my class with Professor DeLure."

Her voice trailed off as she remembered. "I had it in my pack at the party. I put the pack under the sofa we'd been sitting on while we danced, and. . . .

"Perri!"

Anna jumped. "Perri? Perri what?"

"Perri was there. At the party. You remember, I told you how she came up to me and Dare and acted like such a jerk."

"Do you think Perri did this?"

"She had the opportunity. And the motive. I mean, she's dead jealous of me because of Dare."

"Caryl, face it. You and Perri have never gotten along. Not since the moment you met. Do you honestly think her seeing you with Dare would make her start this hate campaign against you?"

"No. Yes. I don't know. But remember, they have a history of some sort. I mean, I get the feeling Perri and Dare were more than just — friends. At least for awhile. Maybe Dare's the one who ended it. You know what they say about the fury of a woman scorned."

"Hmmph. I don't believe in all that *Fatal Attraction* stuff," Anna said firmly. She paused. "And if you do, it applies to Ben as well, wouldn't you say? Have you seen him since your date from hell?"

"No. It's odd. I haven't seen him or heard from him." Caryl gasped. "Ben! I remember now! Perri said something about Ben being at the party. I didn't see him. Did you?"

"No, but it was a big party and I left early."

"So maybe Ben got to the notebook. I mean,

it's not a big secret I keep one. Almost everybody in Professor DeLure's class does. He suggested we do it at the first class."

Caryl felt a surge of anger. "God, I'll kill Ben if it's him. And what if he read some of the stuff I wrote? About him, about me, about Dare, about, oh, about everything! I'll *die*."

Then she heard what she was saying and looked down at the nasty scrawl in her ruined notebook:

Teacher's pet is going to die.

And she heard Giselle's voice:

"Death. . . . beware . . . beware."

Caryl looked at Anna. "Whoever it is, I'm going to find out. And when I do, I'm gonna kill 'em."

I'm gonna kill 'em, the words echoed in her head.

If they don't kill me first.

"He's not there," said Caryl, turning to face Anna. "He called a few days ago. Said he was sick."

"Sick," murmured Anna, "might just describe him."

Caryl and Anna were standing in the post office. Caryl had tried to reach Ben the night before, but he hadn't been in his room. After a long and virtually sleepless night, she'd decided to track him down in the post office. Ben never missed work.

Except he had. "That's not like Ben," she said aloud.

"You don't know that," Anna pointed out. "The Ben you know isn't the real Ben. Maybe."

"Maybe."

"Maybe you should talk to Perri."

"I'm going to talk to Ben first," said Caryl stubbornly. "Then, if, and it's a big if, *if* I believe him, I'll talk to Perri. Meanwhile, I'm going to go back over to Griswold and see if Professor DeLure is in his office yet."

"Count me out this time around," said Anna. "I get enough of the good Professor during class."

Caryl rolled her eyes. "Don't worry. I think I can handle this myself."

Anna paused at the top of the stairs to the post office and gestured. "You sure? It's getting kinda late. Almost dinnertime. I guess I could make the supreme sacrifice and come with you."

"Forget it. I'll be fine."

When Anna looked unconvinced, Caryl gave her a little push in the direction of the library. "You have a test to study for, remember? Besides, you've done enough for one day. I'll catch you later tonight? Okay?"

"Okay," said Anna. "If you're sure."

"I'm sure, I'm sure!"

The two parted, Anna in the direction of the library and Caryl toward Griswold Hall.

Mounting the stairs to the fourth floor, Caryl felt her heart grow lighter despite everything that had happened. She looked forward to seeing Professor DeLure. Trusted him. Believed, somehow that he could make everything come out all right.

But he wasn't there.

She knocked on the door. When no one answered, she gave it a little push. It was firmly closed.

But was it locked?

She tried the door knob. No.

That probably meant he had just stepped out. That he would be coming back soon. Maybe she could wait.

Or maybe he was inside and hadn't even heard her knock.

"Déjà vu," she muttered, remembering her first visit to Professor DeLure's office. But that had been different.

She raised her voice slightly. "Professor DeLure? It's me. Caryl Amberly."

No one answered. Caryl pushed the door wider and stepped into the office. She more than half expected to see Professor DeLure sitting in his chair, absorbed in his thoughts.

But no one was there — except the Siamese fighting fish.

"I'll leave him a message," she said aloud. "It's what I should have done in the first place." Gingerly, being careful not to disturb the stacks of papers and the books tented one atop the other everywhere on the desk's surface, she searched until she found a piece of paper and a pen.

Dear Professor DeLure, she wrote, and stopped.

Her eyes roamed the room. It seemed duller, greyer, without the Professor in it. Of course, she thought, that might also be due to the fact that it was getting dark.

She wrote, *I need to talk to you. It's important. Something strange is going on and I don't know what to do anymore. I hope you can help me* and stopped again. How did one say this: help me stop the crazy person who's been threatening my life. Leaving me dead fish. Following me?

With an impatient gesture, she wadded up the note and threw it in the wastebasket.

She looked around the office again. Then, almost against her will, she went around the desk and sat in Professor DeLure's chair.

This was what it was like to be Professor

DeLure. This was his window, his chair, his desk, his view. She studied the paintings on the wall, somber washes of color, a poster of a swirling, surrealistic painting of a man screaming by an artist named Edward Munch.

She shuddered. Ugh.

Then she noticed the door.

She'd noticed it before. A heavy door with a curious ornate handle. It had always been tightly closed.

But it wasn't now.

What was behind that door? Probably just a closet, thought Caryl, rising to her feet. She walked over and tried the handle.

It opened as easily as the door to Professor DeLure's office had.

Caryl hesitated only a moment. Then she stepped inside.

She blinked.

By a dim light glowing overhead, she saw shelves. Shelves filled with beakers and tubes and bottles and terrariums and aquariums and jars containing things in formaldehyde. A faint, fetid odor clung to the air, as if fresh air from the outside world never reached these depths. A humming sound came from the light overhead. The room was long and dark and narrow, with high ceilings and no window that she could see.

Caryl realized she was standing in a small, private laboratory. Professor DeLure's.

Horrified, apprehensive, fascinated, she stepped closer to one of the shelves. And recoiled.

A human hand? Was that a human hand in one of the jars?

It couldn't be.

She turned quickly away, and gulped. Something that she was almost sure was an eyeball was looking back at her from another jar. She blinked. The eyeball floated weightless, unblinking.

It made the huge, hairy spider her gaze encountered as she turned hastily yet again, seem almost benign.

Except that it wasn't. DANGER was written in large red letters on a sign taped to the terrarium in which the spider reposed. The words TARANTULA and POISONOUS were written below.

The spider was almost as large as her hand. It was covered with black silky fur. As Caryl watched, it lifted something between two black-bristled legs and bit it. Sickened, Caryl realized that the tarantula was eating a live cricket.

"Ugh," she muttered. She began to back away from the sight, and out of the lab.

The spider chewed on. The cricket's legs kicked convulsively.

Caryl's hand touched something cold and she leaped away with a yelp. A terrarium filled with brightly colored stones. Empty. No.

No. Her eyes had deceived her. Motionless as death, a small red, black, and yellow patterned snake curled on the bottom of the terrarium, two tiny, unwinking jeweled eyes staring up at her.

CORAL SNAKE, said the sign. DANGEROUS. Was there nothing in the laboratory that wasn't gruesome, dangerous, or deadly?

Caryl began to turn around slowly, her eyes on the terrariums that were strung along the shelves like lethal fluorescent beads. She had to get out of there without touching anything else. Without turning anything over. Without meeting any of the creatures who waited in their glass prisons.

Slowly, carefully, she turned.

She reached for the door.

The knob turned beneath her hand like a live thing, like a snake or a spider.

She screamed and jerked her hand back. Stumbled and knocked something to the floor. Heard the sound of glass breaking.

The door slammed shut and the light went out.

Chapter 13

For one endless moment, Caryl froze. Then instinctively, she leaped for the door, throwing herself against it.

She hit it with a solid thud. It didn't yield.

"No!" she gasped. "I don't believe this!" Trying to stay calm, she groped for the handle.

But the handle didn't turn in her hand. For a moment, she thought she heard footsteps beyond the door.

"Hello?" she called. She pounded on the door. "There's someone in here! Let me out!"

Then she heard something that chilled her to the bone.

A long, low, laugh. Someone out there was laughing.

Whoever had shut her in this lab of terror had done it intentionally.

And he — or she — thought it was funny.

A wave of panic washed over Caryl.

What had she knocked over? What had she set free in the impenetrable darkness?

She could hear them: Things. Things moving in their terrariums and jars. Things crunching and biting and devouring other living things. Things waiting in the darkness, scrambling through it up out of their glass prisons.

Things slithering and creeping and crawling toward her.

"NOOOOO!" she screamed. She raised her hands and began to beat wildly, insanely, on the door.

"NOOO! HELP ME! HELP ME, PLEASE!

"SOMEBODY PLEEEEEEESE!"

But no one came.

Chapter 14

How long had she pounded on the door with bruised and aching hands? How long had she been trapped in the smothering darkness?

How long had she been waiting, trying in vain to pierce the darkness with her eyes, to see if what she felt touching her legs, her arms, her face, was real.

She couldn't breathe.

She was going mad.

She was dying.

Faintly, she heard the sound of footsteps again. Had whoever locked her in heard her? Realized the mistake and come to set her free?

"It's me!" she sobbed. "It's Caryl. Let me out! Let me out!"

The footsteps stopped. As if someone were on the other side of the door. Listening.

"Please," she pleaded. "Please, help me."

The silence on the other side of the door lengthened. Had she imagined the footsteps?

Something touched her ankle. She leapt away and felt the cool brush of glass against her skin — the glass of one of the terrariums or one of the jars.

But which one? Was it only an eyeball that she had knocked to the floor? Or something living?

Her senses reeled. In another moment, she would be sliding into unconsciousness. Sliding down toward the floor where the things slithered and crept and crawled . . .

The thought jerked her upright for one last effort.

Gathering all her strength, she flung herself shoulder first at the door, flung herself with all her might and the strength of all her terror.

And the door gave way. Opened as if it had never been shut fast against her.

She fell out into the Professor's office.

Into more darkness.

But there was a square of light, a square of wonderful light coming from the office door that opened into the hall. Staggering, gasping, Caryl reeled toward the door.

And fell back with a cry of horror as a figure loomed above her.

Hands caught her arms. She fought wildly, but it was useless.

Then she realized that a voice was saying her name. A familiar voice.

"Dare!" she gasped, "Oh Dare!" And she flung herself into his arms.

"Shhh, shhh," he murmured holding her. "Shhh. It's okay."

"The spider. It ate a cricket. I was locked in . . ."

"Calm down, it's okay."

After a minute she took a deep, shaky breath. "I, it's, I'm better now."

Keeping one arm around her shoulders, Dare reached out with his free hand and flipped on the light. Then he helped Caryl sit down in the leather chair where she had sat talking to Professor DeLure. So recently. So long ago.

"What happened?" asked Dare.

"I came up here to talk to Professor De-Lure," Caryl began, trying to keep her voice steady. "He wasn't here, but his door was open. I thought I'd leave him a message. Then I noticed this other door." Caryl stopped and took a deep breath. "I went in. It's some kind of awful lab . . . with specimens in jars — and *spiders*."

"The spiders scared you."

Caryl sat up indignantly. "No! I mean, not really. But when I turned to leave, someone slammed the door and locked me in and turned off the lights."

"Whoaaaa," Dare breathed. "But — if the door was locked, how did you get out? Are you sure?"

"Yes! Of course I'm sure! Whoever it was must have come back and unlocked it."

But that doesn't make sense, a voice inside her head reminded her. She remembered the laugh.

Unless whoever it was just wanted to scare her. Unless this was some kind of *warning*.

Caryl drew back. "Dare. What are *you* doing here?"

"That's the thanks I get for saving you," complained Dare.

"You didn't save me! I saved myself!"

"Ouch," said Dare. "You're bruising my ego."

"And you're not answering my question. What are you *doing* here?"

"I was on my way to the caf and thought I'd stop by and drop off an assignment early," Dare said. "Satisfied?"

"Oh." Caryl leaned back.

Suddenly an angry voice from the door made them both jump.

"What is the meaning of this?"

"Professor DeLure! N-Nicholas! Oh, I'm so glad to see you!" cried Caryl.

"Are you?" asked Professor DeLure. "Forgive me if I don't say the same, but I'd like to know what you are doing in my office!"

Once again, Caryl told her story. As she did, the Professor's face grew darker and darker. Finishing, Caryl held her breath, expecting an explosion. She had never seen that expression on Professor DeLure's face before, or, for that matter, on anyone else's.

It was murderous. It made Caryl remember what Anna called him.

The Prince of Evil.

But the Professor merely nodded when she was through and turned his head slightly to address Nicholas in a surprisingly mild voice. "Check out the laboratory, Nicholas."

"But, Professor!"

"Do as I say. And be careful."

Nicholas moved slowly away. When he was in the lab, Professor DeLure turned back to Caryl.

"I'm sorry this happened, my dear. The door has an automatic lock on it to prevent anyone from just walking in, for obvious reasons. The light is also on a timer. Clearly there was some malfunction. We'll take care of it right away."

"Malfunction?" Caryl shook her head. "Look at these." She lifted her backpack and reached inside and pulled out her notebook and the threatening poem that had come wrapped around the dead fish. She handed them to Professor DeLure. As he read them, she told him about the dead Siamese fighting fish in her mailbox.

"Ah," he said with menacing softness. He looked at her for a long moment. "I see."

He folded the note and put it in his pocket. "I will keep this, if you don't mind. I'll return your notebook to you, but do not lose it," he commanded. "I'll speak to Professor Perez. Be assured, this matter will be taken care of."

"I'm not sure who's responsible, really," said Caryl. "At first I thought it might be someone who . . . who I used to go out with. But now I don't know."

"The matter will be taken care of," Professor DeLure repeated.

Nicholas came back into the office, his face pale. Caryl noticed he was wearing heavy leather gloves.

"You were lucky, Caryl," he said, his voice

hoarse. "One of the terrariums is open, somehow. Some of the spiders were out."

"The tarantula," she breathed fearfully.

Nicholas paused and took a deep breath. His eyes met the Professor's.

Then Nicholas went on. "Yes. You're lucky you weren't bitten. They can be quite aggressive. And their bite can be, at best, unpleasant."

"The Tarantella," murmured the Professor.

"Yes," said Nicholas. His face was pale. "It's a dance named after the spider. Some call it — the dance of death."

"Are you okay?" asked Dare.

"I don't know," answered Caryl wearily. She'd never felt so tired. So alone. And in spite of Dare's presence, she couldn't shake the feeling that she was being followed, watched.

"Who do you think is behind you?" Dare asked quietly as Caryl tried unobtrusively to look over her shoulder for what felt like the hundredth time since leaving Griswold Hall. The campus was dark and quiet behind her.

She shrugged and slid her hand into Dare's for comfort. "I don't know. I don't know what to think anymore. I guess it could have been an accident, me getting locked in that lab. But I can't make myself believe it." She looked up at Dare, her eyes desolate. "I'm really beginning to believe someone is out to get me. And you know what's worse? I think it's someone close to me, someone who knows me. Someone who pretends to like me — but who really hates me."

They'd reached the Quad. "This is where I leave you," said Dare. "I wish it wasn't." He put his hand against Caryl's cheek and gave her a quick kiss. "You call me," he said. "If anything comes up, no matter how small, no matter how unimportant it seems, you call me. And if I don't hear from you, I'll call you, okay?"

Dare's concern made Caryl feel a little better and she managed to give him what must have passed for a normal smile, because he smiled back, looking relieved.

"I'm not going to tell you not to worry, Caryl . . ."

"Good . . ."

"But I'm going to help you figure this thing out."

"Thank you, Dare."

"Good night," he said.

"G'night." She turned and walked up the stairs to the Quad Main entrance.

I know I'm being watched now, she thought and held her head high. Stepping in the door, she turned.

Sure enough, Dare was watching, making sure she got inside safely.

"Tomorrow," he said.

"Tomorrow," she agreed.

But tomorrow seemed a long, long way away.

Chapter 15

Half a dozen girls were gathered in Anna's room when Caryl stopped by. Anna was passing a bowl of popcorn and she didn't seem to notice how out of it Caryl felt. Maybe, thought Caryl, it doesn't show.

She couldn't decide if that was good or bad.

"Come on in," called Anna cheerfully. "We're having a pigout."

"No thanks," said Caryl.

"How'd it go?" asked Anna. "Here, will someone take this popcorn off my hands? Who's got the chips?"

"It was — different," said Caryl wryly.

"Did you get to talk to our favorite killer-diller professor?"

"Yes. He said he'd take care of the note and everything."

"Cool," Anna said. "So come on in. We have enough junk food to take your mind off all your worries. Really. The party's just getting started."

"Yeah, we're just about to start telling ghost stories. It's a Salem tradition, you know. Think of Nightmare Hall," someone said.

"Right," said Anna. "Giselle. The girl who died at Nightmare Hall. She's the resident ghost now, right?"

"I've never heard it was *haunted*, exactly," someone else said.

Caryl groped for the doorjamb and grabbed it in a death grip. "Did you say Giselle?" she croaked.

At last Anna seemed to notice that Caryl was not herself. "Caryl? Are you okay?"

"Is that what you said? Giselle?"

Anna looked surprised. "Yes. Giselle. The girl who was killed in Nightingale Hall last spring."

"I've gotta go," said Caryl, turning blindly away. "I've . . . I'll talk to you later."

Caryl blundered out into the hall, scarcely seeing where she was going. It wasn't possible. It couldn't be. It couldn't have happened.

But it had.

Caryl had been talking to a ghost.

A ghost who had warned her.

A ghost who had warned her of her own death.

A ghost.

It couldn't be true.

No one would believe her.

But it had happened.

"Oh, my God," moaned Caryl, "oh my God. I'm going to die."

The next few days were a nightmare for Caryl. Dare called, but she didn't want to see him. Anna hovered solicitously, but her constant "Are you okay?" made Caryl nervous. Nor did Ben's conspicuous absence make her feel better.

She felt as if she were being watched, followed, whispered about, and the thought of Ben lurking somewhere just out of her line of sight did not calm her.

"Caryl. Ms. Amberly!"

Walking slowly across campus one afternoon, Caryl looked up to see Professor DeLure.

"I'm glad I see you here. I wanted to speak with you before our next class." The Professor paused and studied her keenly. "You don't look well."

Caryl managed a wan smile. "I'm fine."

Something in the Professor's intent scrutiny reminded Caryl of Anna. She turned her head away slightly, hoping that he couldn't read the exhaustion and fear in her face.

"I'm not sure I believe you. However, I do want to reassure you. I have spoken to Professor Perez about these notes and she is taking steps. I can also assure you that the ghastly accident of being locked inside the laboratory by my office will never happen to anyone again. *I* have taken steps to deal with that."

"Good," said Caryl haltingly. "I'm glad."

"But you are letting all this affect you, are you not?" asked Professor DeLure.

"No! No, really, I'm fine. It's just been kind of a tough week. You know."

Professor DeLure did not look entirely convinced, but at length he said, "Well. I'll see you in class then, Caryl."

"Yes," Caryl answered dully, and trudged on.

If she didn't look up, if she didn't talk to anybody, then they couldn't meet her eyes. And if she didn't see anyone watching her, then it was almost as if it wasn't happening.

Right.

"Caryl!" For the second time that day, someone called Caryl's name. She halted wearily, and waited without turning.

"Caryl, I saw you with Professor DeLure." It was Nicholas.

He drew alongside her and paused. When

Caryl didn't answer, Nicholas said, "What did the Professor say?"

"He said he'd taken care of everything," said Caryl. She began walking again. Keep moving, she thought vaguely. It's harder to hit a moving target.

"Caryl, are you listening to me?" Nicholas's voice brought her back rudely to reality.

She was beginning to hate reality.

"Caryl, I think you should come with me."

"What for?" She kept walking.

"I can't tell you. I'll have to show you."

"Show me what?"

Nicholas grabbed her arm and gave her a shake. "This is important!"

Some spark of energy returned at Nicholas's rough treatment. She yanked her arm free. "This sounds like a bad line, Nicholas."

"Will you come on!"

"Let go of me."

Something in her tone reached Nicholas. He released her arm. "It's important," he repeated. "You have to believe me."

"I don't have to do anything," she answered. *Except maybe die.*

"Will you come with me? Please?"

Something in Nicholas's tone reached her.

"All right," she said at last.

But when they reached Griswold Hall, she

stopped again. She hadn't been back since the night she'd been locked in the lab. She wasn't sure she could make herself go in now.

Nicholas took her arm again. His voice was urgent. "Come on! We have to do this now, while the Professor is away from his office. We don't have much time."

Reluctantly, she allowed him to pull her along, into the old brick building and up the endless flights of stairs. At the end of each flight her heart thundered more loudly in her ears. By the time they reached Professor DeLure's office door, she couldn't think for the roaring, fearful pounding.

She was afraid.

But she forced herself not to show it.

Nicholas took out a key and opened the office door.

In spite of herself, Caryl flinched as he drew her inside.

She didn't know what she expected. What she thought she'd see.

But it looked just the same. Ordinary. Harmless.

"The lab door has been secured, see?" said Nicholas motioning, and Caryl saw a round lock had been set into the wood. Nicholas drew her forward, around Professor DeLure's desk. He took out another key and unlocked the desk.

"What are you doing?" asked Caryl.

Nicholas didn't answer. He re-pocketed the key, opened the bottom drawer, reached far into the back and took out a silver-framed photograph.

"I think you better take a look at this." He laid the picture carefully on the desk in front of Caryl.

For a moment, Caryl's eyes wouldn't focus. Then she realized she was staring down at an old photograph of a young woman, about her own age.

A young woman with blonde hair and laughing eyes dressed in a sweater that matched her eyes, trying to look solemn for the photographer and not entirely succeeding.

Caryl reached out wonderingly and touched the photograph. "How did you get this?" she asked. "How did you get this picture of *me*?"

Chapter 16

Gently, Nicholas took the framed photograph from Caryl's hand and laid it on the desk.

"It's not you, Caryl. You know that, don't you?"

"I — " Caryl stared down at the photograph. She realized it was true. It wasn't her. Those weren't her clothes. They were too old-fashioned, too out-of-style for her to have ever worn. And she had never worn her hair that way.

But everything else was the same. It was like looking in a mirror.

"I — I don't understand," she said at last.

"Her name is Claire. Claire DeLure. She was Professor DeLure's daughter."

A chill crept up Caryl's spine. "Is this some kind of a joke, Nicholas? Because if it is . . ."

"No joke," said Nicholas. "Listen to me, Caryl. Professor DeLure isn't like he is because he was born that way. It's because of Claire. Because of the way she died."

He stared down at the photograph, his face somber. "Professor DeLure killed her. And now — "

Nicholas stopped. He raised his eyes from the photograph to Caryl's face.

My face, thought Caryl. Claire's face.

Suddenly she didn't want to hear what Nicholas was going to say. With an inarticulate cry, she pushed him away, and ran out of the office.

The phone was ringing. Ringing and ringing and ringing.

With a groan Caryl buried her head deeper under the covers.

The ringing stopped.

A hand touched her shoulder through the blankets and in spite of herself, Caryl gave a muffled shriek, flinging the covers back and practically leaping up.

Anna jumped back, her expression startled.

"Chill, Caryl. It's just me. I hadn't talked to you today and I came by to see if you're okay."

"I'm okay! Okay?"

Anna studied Caryl for a moment.

As if I was some kind of bug or specimen she's dissecting, thought Caryl.

Then Anna said, "Well, if you're so okay, you've got a phone call."

"I'm not here," said Caryl, turning back toward the refuge of the blankets.

"It's Nicholas," said Anna, her face oddly blank. "He said he's been calling and calling. That it's important."

"Forget it."

"Caryl." Anna's voice was uncharacteristically flat. "I said, you have a phone call. It's Nicholas France. I'm not going to lie for you and say you're not here. Understand?"

"Oh, all right!"

Furiously, Caryl stalked across the room and picked up the phone.

"What?" she almost shouted into it.

Nicholas's voice, almost as agitated as hers, said, "Caryl. I've got to see you. Got to talk to you."

"Well I don't want to see you," said Caryl.

"We've got to talk. You didn't let me finish. You've got to let me explain."

"No."

"Listen to me. *Listen to me*. It's a matter of life and death!"

In the act of taking the phone away from her ear, of slamming it down, Caryl stopped.

Beware . . .

Death.

"Caryl?"

"I'm here."

Beware . . .

"I need to talk to you."

"Okay. Okay, Nicholas, I'll see you. Tomorrow."

"Tomorrow!" protested Nicholas.

"You're the one who wants to see me," Caryl reminded him rudely. "So be at Morte par Chocolat. At one."

Caryl hung up the phone without waiting for an answer, her face grim.

But it was no grimmer than Anna's.

"Nicholas, too?" said Anna with steel in her voice.

"What are you talking about Anna?"

"I'm talking about you and Dare. You and poor Ben. And now you and Nicholas. How much is enough for you?"

"Anna, please. Whatever it is you're imagining, it isn't true. I'm having a hard time right now."

"You're having a hard time. Is this what you do to handle the hard times? Betray your friends?"

"I'm not betraying anybody!"

"I'm supposed to be your friend. Your *best friend*. You knew, you *know* I — like — Nicholas. But that hasn't stopped you, has it? *You* had to go after him too. God, you make Perri look like an angel!"

"What! Are you crazy?"

"Me?" Anna shook her head. "Oh, no, *I'm* not crazy."

Caryl jerked back as if she'd been slapped. "Anna!"

"How could you do this to me? To *me*? I hate you, Caryl! Hate you, hate you, hate you!"

Anna turned and ran from the room.

"Anna?"

Caryl rapped lightly on Anna's door. She'd given her an hour to unwind. Now it was time to talk. To explain.

She needed Anna's help.

But no one answered.

"Anna?" Caryl tried again.

"She's not here," a sleepy voice inside the room said.

"Sorry," Caryl called back to Anna's roommate.

Where could Anna be?

She went back to her room. What was she going to do?

She couldn't believe this was happening.

"I'll call Dare," she said aloud. The sound of the words reassured her. At least Dare would listen. He would understand. He could help.

Dare wasn't home. She left a message for him.

But although she stayed awake long into the night, tossing and turning on the edge of nightmares, listening, hoping for the phone to ring, he never called her back.

She got to Morte par Chocolat early and found a table in the corner. She took the chair with the back to the wall, where she could watch everybody coming and going.

I'm not paranoid, she thought. Oh, no, not a bit. She drew a ragged breath and motioned to the waiter.

It was the same waiter who'd gone so dippy over Perri. The memory almost made Caryl smile. Almost.

"Espresso," she ordered. "No, wait. Make that a double."

Morte par Chocolat hummed along on the usual swirl of muted, intense conversations, sudden bursts of laughter, and the smell of coffee and chocolate and steamy windows. The day had turned colder and Caryl watched the shadowy forms beyond the misted glass hurry along the sidewalk, bulky in sweaters and coats against the chill, bent forward into the sudden gusts of wind. The restaurant felt cozy and safe.

Except that it wasn't. No place was safe anymore.

Caryl accepted the tiny cup of bitter black brew from the waiter gratefully and drank a scalding sip. It burnt her tongue and seared her senses and she was glad.

This was where it all began, she thought suddenly. The day I got into Professor De-Lure's class and came here with Anna.

That is when all my trouble began.

Nicholas came in the door and paused and spotted Caryl.

He lifted his hand in greeting but she didn't return the welcome. She watched him impassively as he crossed the restaurant and slid into the chair across from her.

The waiter appeared and hovered expectantly.

"Coffee," said Nicholas briefly. "Plain old coffee."

With a sniff of disapproval, the waiter slid away.

Nicholas grinned awkwardly. "I just can't drink that stuff," he said, indicating Caryl's espresso. "Too much for me."

"What do you want, Nicholas?"

The grin left Nicholas's face. "Right. Okay, listen. Everyone knows all the rumors about the Professor. I assume you do too."

Caryl nodded, giving him nothing.

"Well, I have too. That he killed his daughter, that he killed his wife, the whole bit. I didn't believe any of it, of course. Not then.

"I mean, Professor DeLure is a brilliant man, a genius. He's also impatient with people who aren't as smart as he is. That kind of thing makes you enemies.

"But then I found that picture in his desk. And then I saw you. And Professor DeLure starting behaving — strangely. So I started doing a little homework. And I found out that he *had* killed his daughter."

"I don't believe you," said Caryl, struggling to control her voice. "It's not possible."

"It's true. They said it was an accident. It's how he lost his eye. A car wreck. He blamed himself." Nicholas paused. "My God, who wouldn't?"

They were both silent for a moment. The waiter appeared with the coffee and Nicholas absently stirred in some cream.

Then he went on. "Anyway, I think when he saw you, Caryl, it brought it all back to him. All the guilt and pain and anger. And I think he just sort of snapped."

"And?" She'd regained control now. *I can take it*, she thought.

"I think you haunt him. I think he's beginning to confuse you with his daughter. I think it is happening more and more and that he's beginning to fear you. To hate you. I think he's obsessed with you, Caryl. I'm afraid he's going to lose control. That something terrible is going to happen."

Nicholas stopped.

Through stiff lips, Caryl said, "To me."

Slowly, Nicholas nodded.

Caryl drank the rest of her espresso in one burning gulp and clattered the cup down in her saucer. A thousand thoughts crossed her mind: the Professor's attention to her, his kindness. His reaction the first day he'd seen her. The dead Siamese fighting fish. The notes.

The way it had all begun that day she got into Professor DeLure's class. That day she'd gone to visit him in his office.

"I don't believe you," she said. But her voice lacked conviction.

She stood up and dropped some money on the table. "I don't. I've got to go."

"What are you going to do?" asked Nicholas, standing too, as if to stop her. "Don't do anything random, anything crazy."

"Crazy?" said Caryl. She laughed and she knew it wasn't a normal laugh. "Don't worry about me. Now, if you'll excuse me, I have a class to get to. You might know about it — it's a poetry class for scientists. Or something like that." She picked up her pack and walked to the door of the restaurant.

And into Dare.

"Whoa!"

"Dare!"

"Hi, Caryl. Sorry about that."

"It's okay." Caryl bent to gather up her backpack and the pencils and pens that had spilled out of one of the half-zipped compartments. Dare bent to help her.

"So where's the fire?" asked Dare.

"What?"

"What's your hurry?"

"I have class," said Caryl, forgetting Dare was in the same class with her. "With Professor DeLure." She stood up, zipping her pack. "Thanks."

Dare looked at his watch, then looked at her. "You've got plenty of time."

"Oh." Caryl shrugged. "Well." Somehow, she wanted to lead Dare away from Morte par Chocolat, away from any questions he might ask about why she was there and who she was there with. She started walking.

"Dare?" she said, realizing that he hadn't fallen into step beside her.

Dare was staring through the steam-clouded doors of the coffee shop. When she called his name he turned quickly. His face was devoid of expression.

"I'll walk with you," he said. "So, what's happening?"

I tried to call you last night and you weren't there, she thought wearily. Did you have a date with Perri?

"Not much," she said aloud. She didn't feel like telling him what Nicholas had said. Saying it aloud to Dare, to anyone, would make it more real.

And might make her believe it.

She drifted back to campus with Dare, holding up her end of the conversation without knowing what she was saying. Fortunately, Dare didn't seem to notice her distraction. And the chill gave her a chance to keep the collar of her jacket turned up so that he couldn't really see her face.

She took a seat in the back of the class.

"What's this?" teased Dare. "Giving up the front row seat? Trying to duck your favorite prof? Don't you have your homework?"

"Yes! I mean, no. Not exactly." Forcing herself to smile a big, bright, happy smile, she added, "It's been a tough week, Dare. You know that. I guess I kinda let some things slide."

Dare reached out and tugged a strand of her

hair gently. "Hey, anytime you need help with your homework, you know who to call."

"Hey, you know I will," she answered.

"You're in my seat," Perri drawled sarcastically, sauntering up to Caryl. "But that's okay. Stay there."

With that, she followed Dare, sliding into the seat next to him.

The rest of the class had drifted in, with Professor DeLure on their heels. The Professor closed the classroom door and went to the front of the room. He leaned back against the desk, crossed his ankles, folded his arms, and surveyed the class. Seeing Caryl in the back, a small frown appeared in his eye, but he made no comment. Instead, he held them all silent under his scrutiny for a moment longer. Then he began to talk.

Caryl sensed the others being caught up as usual in his spell. But for once, the magic wasn't working for Caryl.

Maybe it never would again.

She studied Professor DeLure. Tried to see him with the detached eye of a scientist. Her hero. Her mentor.

Could what Nicholas said be true? Could that be the explanation behind everything that had happened? Could the Professor be the one who had sent her those crude poems? Who had killed a Siamese fighting fish and left it in the damp package in the post office? Locked her in the lab with the spiders?

Could he possibly believe that she was his daughter, come back to haunt him? To get revenge?

But she couldn't believe that the Professor who had been so kind, so generous with his time, the Professor who had told her she had talent and had encouraged her, could be like that.

Unless he was a monster. A Dr. Jekyll and Mr. Hyde. A man without a conscience.

A man who hadn't killed his daughter by accident. Who had . . . *murdered* her.

And who would murder Caryl, too.

No.

No, there had to be a logical explanation for it all. A rational one, as Anna would say.

Anna. Unexpectedly jealous Anna. Anna, who, like Ben, was now avoiding her.

Could Anna have been hiding a split personality all along? A deeper jealousy than her jealousy over Nicholas?

That wasn't possible. Or logical. Or rational.

Anna was Anna, nobody else.

Unbidden, the thought of Dare crept into her brain. Mysterious Dare.

Was it possible Dare had something to hide?

Why *was* he always so conveniently on the spot when things happened: her getting locked in the lab; her coffee meeting with Nicholas.

But there was no reason for Dare to hate her, to want to scare her, to harm her. No reason at all.

Unless he was truly crazy.

Caryl realized she was trembling.

Stop it, she ordered herself. *Stay calm. Think.*

Ben, then. Ben, who definitely had a hidden, dark side. That's who it was. That's who it had to be. Ben. Ben, who was hiding from her now. Ben, who was probably the one who was making her feel followed, watched. Maybe Ben had —

"Ms. Amberly?"

Startled, Caryl looked around. She swallowed hard. "I'm sorry. Could you repeat the question?"

The Professor looked disappointed, but he only said, "That's quite all right. We'll move along."

Someone in the room snickered. Perri, of course.

Hateful, hate-filled Perri. Perri, who wanted Caryl to fail. Who hated Caryl for Dare's attention to her. Perri, who would do anything to get her way. Any wicked thing.

Perri.

Maybe even, Perri and Ben. Look at how easily Perri twisted people around her finger. Maybe she'd done that to Ben. Maybe Perri and Ben were in this together.

The end-of-class chimes began to toll from the Salem tower, startling Caryl from her reverie. On the last stroke of the chimes, the Professor picked up a stack of manila envelopes. "Some readings I've compiled for you for next week."

"Do you want me to do that, Professor DeLure?" asked Nicholas, stepping to the front of the room. But the Professor was already passing the envelopes down the rows.

Nicholas stepped back. His eyes swept the room as if he were searching for someone. They widened a little when he saw Caryl.

Like he didn't know I was going to be here, she thought, and felt a little spurt of anger. What does he think I am, a coward? A quitter? I'm not.

"If you'll read this material for next week," the Professor began. Caryl opened hers and slid it out obediently. But she didn't get to look at what the Professor had given her.

A horrible shriek filled the room. Perri leaped up from her desk, dancing madly, shaking her hand and screaming. Her desk fell over backwards with a crash.

"AAAAAAAH!" she howled, her gyrations becoming frantic, insane. "ITBITMEITBIT MEGET IT OFFME!"

She stumbled, suddenly clumsy. The scream died in her throat. Her eyes rolled back in her head and her jaw grew slack and she fell to the floor like a corpse.

Chapter 17

Dare, who was closest, leapt up to help Perri.

But the Professor's voice stopped him.

"Stand back!" he said. "Don't move. Nobody move!"

Everyone froze. The Professor took a thick handkerchief out of his pocket and walked swiftly forward. "Stay where you are. Everyone. Stay where you are."

Holding the handkerchief in front of him, he bent over Perri. He examined her inert form for what seemed like an eternity.

Then, like a snake striking, his hand shot out. He stood up.

"Call an ambulance, Nicholas," he ordered curtly over his shoulder.

For one moment, Caryl's attention was drawn to Nicholas. He was standing there, his mouth open, his eyes wide with horror.

"Did you hear me, Nicholas? Now!"

Like a man waking from a nightmare, Nicholas jumped, and swallowed convulsively. Then he said, "Yes. Okay."

He ran toward the door.

The Professor's voice stopped him. "And Nicholas? Tell them to bring an antidote for poison." He lifted his hand and opened his handkerchief and held it out. A crushed, horrible, hairy object twitched in its death throes in the middle of the white material. "Tarantula poison."

Nicholas turned and ran from the room.

Caryl swayed and would have fallen had her desk not been right behind her. She sat down hard. Murmurs of conversation had broken out in the room, but she lowered her head, unhearing, unseeing.

All she could see was Perri's still, still form, lying on the floor, with Professor DeLure kneeling again beside her.

Perri was sitting in my usual seat, Caryl thought suddenly.

That spider was meant for me.

It wasn't Perri who was out to get me after all, thought Caryl. It couldn't have been.

Her eyes went to Professor DeLure. His head was bent. He seemed to be studying the crushed body of the spider in his handkerchief.

It wasn't Perri, thought Caryl. It was Professor DeLure.

"Anna, please! You've got to talk to me!"

The phone went dead.

Caryl dialed again.

Someone picked it up at the other end. And slammed it down.

Defeated, Caryl hung up the phone.

"The spiders are coming, the spiders are coming."

It was Anna's voice. Caryl sat up in the darkness. She groped for the light, then jerked her hand back. What if there were spiders on the lamp?

What if there were spiders in the bed with her?

She started to call out for her roommate, then remembered that Phyllis had left for a long weekend at home.

She was alone in the room.

Except for the spiders.

"Anna," she said.

Someone laughed softly. Mockingly. "You all look alike when you're dead," a voice hissed.

Where was it coming from?

With a desperate effort, Caryl forced herself to reach out and turn on the light.

Her room leaped into view, a little messy, filled with the comforting clutter of her life.

I was dreaming, she thought.

Then she looked over at Phyllis's bed. She *was* there. Caryl could see her sleeping form under the blanket. Had she decided to wait to leave until tomorrow? But that wasn't possible. Caryl had seen her leave, suitcase in hand.

She leaned forward slightly to peer at the sleeping shape on the bed.

Phyllis's face looked back at her from the pillow.

Phyllis's face, blackened, swollen, her tongue protruding between her lips, one eye glistening horribly with death and pain.

Over the other eye, a gruesome black thing sat, hairy and huge.

A spider.

Caryl began to scream and scream and scream.

"Hey! Hey, what's going on in there!"

Pounding on the door.

Caryl bolted up, her mouth still open.

"Hey," the voice called. "Are you okay? Unlock the door!"

"Just — just a minute." Caryl reached out, hesitated, then flipped on the light.

Her room came into view, a little messy,

filled with all the comforting clutter of her life.

Fearfully, Caryl glanced toward her roommate's bed.

It was neatly made. Empty.

She stumbled toward the door and opened it. Lacey Sakurada from down the hall stood there. "Are you, like, okay? You were screaming loud enough to wake the dead."

Caryl ran her tongue over her lips and laughed weakly. "Nightmare," she croaked.

"Oh. Well, it sounded world-class. You want some company or something?"

"No. Thanks. Sorry about that."

"No problem," said Lacey. "I was up anyway." She left and Caryl closed the door behind her. She leaned against it, closing her eyes, trying to get her bearings.

"Air," she thought, "I need some air."

She stumbled to the window and fumbled it open and leaned out into the chill darkness, taking deep breaths.

Then her breath stopped in her throat.

Her room faced out over the campus. And across the street, in the shadow of one of the ancient oaks that dotted the campus, she saw a darker shadow.

A shadow shaped like a person.

Knowing she was silhouetted clearly against the light in her room, Caryl tried to step back casually. She raised her arms, pretending to yawn. She closed the window and walked back across the room and turned off the light.

Then, as quickly as she could, she hurried back to the window and leaned against the wall next to it and peered around the edge.

The shadow was still there. Still watching. She watched the shadow for a long, long time. Counted out the lazy strokes of the tower clock marking the passing of another late hour.

And finally, finally the shadow detached itself and slid away, into the darker shadows behind the tree, along the edge of a hedge.

And then it was gone.

The pain in her hands made her look down. Her hands were clenched so tightly that her fingernails had made bloody little half-moons in her palms. She unclenched her hands and took a deep breath and felt rage, pure rage, fill her heart.

She remembered an old movie she'd seen. The words came back to her now and she clutched them to herself — a motto, a challenge to the darkness that seemed to be grasping at her from every side.

"I'm mad as hell," she muttered. "I'm not going to take this anymore."

Chapter 18

The next morning, Caryl got up early and dressed carefully. She felt as if she were donning armor for battle — if, she thought wryly, my favorite shirt and jeans can be called armor. She laced up her Doc Martens, put a leather vest on top of the shirt and surveyed herself in the mirror.

The girl that looked back at her was pale but resolute, a fiery spark in her eye and a determined set to her chin.

"I'm on my own," she said aloud, and then remembering what her mother had always said, repeated, "Behind every good woman is herself."

Feeling somehow better, she turned and walked out the door for class.

She was surprised to find that she was able to concentrate after all. It was as if the nightmare and the subsequent anger had freed her somehow. She felt keen, sharp, like the finely honed edge of a knife.

Ready.

Waiting.

She wasn't ready, though, for what happened at the post office.

Although in a way, it now seemed almost a given: to reach in, to pull out magazines, bills, letters from friends — and a folded sheet of paper with the crude printing on it.

She unfolded it and read:

Every move you make
I'll be watching you
You're the next to die, Caryl
And there's nothing you can do.

The next to die. She almost laughed. She raised her chin defiantly. "You're a bad poet," she said aloud. "Do you hear me?"

Realizing that others in the post office were watching her, Caryl stuffed the rest of her mail in her backpack and, with the poem crumpled in her hand, left.

The next to die, she thought. Was Perri dead, then? Perri didn't deserve to be dead — even if Caryl and half of Salem University had felt like killing her more than once.

She rounded the corner of the post office, and stopped short.

Anna and Ben were standing by the post office door, their heads close together, obviously deep in conversation.

Anna and Ben.

Not Perri and Ben. Anna and Ben.

Her confidence fled, leaving her cold and shaken. Slowly, slowly she backed away, willing them not to see her.

Anna and Ben. Was it them, then? Had Ben started it and Anna offered to help him finish? Were they in it together, a little game of Let's Drive Caryl Crazy Or At Least Scare Her to Death?

Anna and Ben.

She bumped into someone, hard.

"We can't keep meeting like this," a familiar, welcome voice complained.

"Dare."

"The one and only. Hey!" He reeled slightly backwards as she impulsively flung her arms around him. "Hey, this is decent. I've changed my mind. We *can* keep meeting like this."

She pulled back. "Okay."

"Feeling better?"

She was startled. So much for armor, she thought. "Yeah," she answered.

"So's Perri," said Dare. "I thought you'd like

to know. She's still alive. They think she's going to make it.

"I'm glad," said Caryl. *The next to die. Perri's not dead yet, so I can't be next.*

She almost giggled.

"You're not okay," said Dare. His eye caught the paper wadded into Caryl's fist. "What's this?"

"Oh, you know. One of those poems." Amazingly enough, her voice was calm.

Without speaking, Dare reached down and opened her fingers and took the piece of paper from them. He smoothed it out and read it.

Then he handed it back to Caryl.

If she expected him to say something about the note, she was wrong. Instead, watching her keenly, he said, "They're saying it was an accident. What happened to Perri. What do you think?"

"What else could it be?" asked Caryl.

Dare shook his head. "I don't know. But I don't think it was an accident. And I'm not sure Perri was the Miss Muffet the spider was intended for."

Why was Dare watching her so closely? What was he trying to say? Caryl waited for him to say more, but he didn't. When she said nothing, he said, abruptly, "Catch you later," and turned and walked away.

She stared after him.

And a little voice began to almost purr in her ear: "What's the matter, Caryl? Did you and Dare have a little fight?"

Caryl wheeled. "Anna! Oh, Anna, am I glad to see you! We've got to talk."

"I can't talk to you, Caryl. I'm too angry."

Anna turned on her heel and strode off, leaving Caryl alone.

"May I please speak to Professor DeLure?"

"He's not here. May I take a message?"

"Who is this?" Caryl demanded.

With a faint note of surprise in her voice, the woman at the other end of the phone said, "I'm the office manager for the Science Department. This is the Science Department Main Office."

"Oh." Caryl felt foolish. "Well, yes, please. I'd like to leave a message." She gave the woman her phone number and said, "I'll be here all day. If I don't hear from him, I'm going to come by his office this evening. I know this is one of the nights he keeps evening hours."

"From 8:00 to 9:00," the woman confirmed. "I'll see that Professor DeLure gets your message."

"Thank you," said Caryl.

She hung up the phone. She checked the door

to her room. It was locked. No way in.

No way out.

Nothing to do now but wait. Wait until it was time to confront Professor Maximillian DeLure.

Chapter 19

The Professor's door was ajar. The rest of the doors on the hall were closed. He was the only one who kept such late office hours for students. The other professors had husbands and wives and partners and families waiting for them at home, he'd said once to Caryl.

Anna had snorted when Caryl told her that. He just doesn't want to be bothered with his students, she'd retorted. He knows no one is going to come around that late.

Anna.

"Professor DeLure," said Caryl, pushing the door open. "Did you get my message? I'm here . . ."

Her voice trailed off.

Professor DeLure was in his chair, facing the window.

"Professor DeLure?"

Slowly the chair swiveled around.

Professor DeLure was dead.

It was worse than her worst nightmare.

His face was grotesquely distorted and unnaturally shiny and red. His tongue protruded between his lips. Flecks of foam had collected in the corners of his mouth. His eyepatch had been pushed askew and the red, empty socket stared out at her. His whole body was rigid.

"Professor DeLure!" She heard her voice going up, up, into the hysterical range. With the greatest effort she'd ever made, she pulled it back down.

"Professor DeLure."

He didn't answer. She hadn't really expected him to. Looking down, anywhere but at his dead, staring eyesocket, she saw that he was holding a small, empty vial in one tightly clutched fist.

"No," whispered Caryl. "No, oh no."

"Oh, yesss," whispered a mocking voice behind her.

Caryl turned.

It was Nicholas France. Nicholas France, looking as sane and friendly and kindly as he always had.

But he wasn't.

"He killed himself," Nicholas said, his voice softly, evilly triumphant. "He killed himself."

"Why?" gasped Caryl.

"Because he knew he deserved to die. He knew that if he didn't take the easy way out, *I* was going to get him."

"You? What are you talking about, Nicholas?" She looked past him toward the door. He laughed.

"You won't be leaving here tonight. You won't be leaving here at all. At least not . . . *alive*."

"Nicholas." She clenched her hands at her sides. "Nicholas, tell me. Tell me what this is all about." .

"You want me to talk," said Nicholas slyly. "You want me to keep talking until someone comes to rescue you, hmmmm? But no one will. No one knows where you are tonight. I took care of that. I left messages for all your friends.

"They think you're at the library. Working on your precious poetry."

"Nicholas."

"I took the message you left for Professor DeLure. I gave it to him. You played right into my hands, Caryl."

"I don't understand, Nicholas. Why?" she asked desperately.

He grinned. Such a pleasant, easy, open grin for a madman to wear.

"He killed her. Claire. She was the only girl I ever loved and he killed her to keep us apart."

A faraway look came into Nicholas's eyes. "He never liked me. I was a student at the college where he taught. That's where I met Claire. She was just in high school. We went out. But the Professor didn't like it. No matter how nice, how polite I was to him, he never liked me.

"He forbade Claire to see me. But Claire loved me. She agreed to one last meeting and I told her my plan. I was going to take her away. Save her. Fix it so we could be together always.

"But *he* was following us. He chased us. I lost control of the car. Claire was killed.

"They said I didn't have a chance of surviving. But they were wrong. I didn't die. Months and months in that hospital, but I didn't die."

He paused, reached up and touched the faint scar along his ear. "I was — disfigured. When I woke up I realized what had happened. I chose a new face. A new me. A new life."

He laughed. And all the craziness, all the insanity that was hidden behind his face came out in the laugh. It was a chilling sound.

"I found the Professor. Of course he didn't recognize me now. I became his most devoted student. And I waited."

"When you came along, I knew that what I'd been waiting for had finally happened. You

— you look so much like *her*. You were the perfect tool, don't you see?"

"No," whispered Caryl.

Nicholas went on, ignoring her. "I made it look like the Professor was obsessed with you. That he was sinking deeper and deeper into madness, believing you were the reincarnation of Claire come back to haunt him. A hint here, a hint there . . . didn't you see it, Caryl? Didn't you see the way people talked, the way they whispered about the Professor's new pet?"

Caryl shook her head mutely.

"I did. I watched. Watched him going mad before my eyes. It was wonderful to see him suffer. To suffer even a little of what I had suffered. To know that he knew something was wrong, but that he was powerless to stop it. Powerless to protect you, to tell you. Powerless to protect himself."

"You sent me those notes?"

"It was easy," Nicholas bragged. "And the Siamese fighting fish — that was a nice touch, don't you think? I was in the lab that day you first came to visit. I'd seen you for the first time with your friend and I'd made a point, from that moment on, to keep an eye on you. To watch you. To know you. I know everything about you."

"*You* were the one following me, watching

me?" Caryl cried. A shudder convulsed her. She hadn't been paranoid. It had been true all along.

Nicholas smiled with satisfaction at her reaction. "I locked you in the lab. And *you* were supposed to get bitten by the death spider, not Perri. But you didn't. You were sitting in the wrong place."

Foolishly, with some vain hope of placating Nicholas, Caryl stammered, "I'm sorry."

"Not as sorry as you're going to be. You see, the Professor, he cooperated very, very nicely. He committed suicide. But I'm afraid I'm going to have to kill you."

"Nicholas."

"It'll look like he did it, then offed himself in remorse. It will be a scandal. The well-respected Professor DeLure . . . won't be so well-respected anymore."

Caryl backed away from Nicholas. She tried to think of a way to escape. But the lab door was locked. And to leap through the windows was to leap to almost certain death four stories below.

She stepped back and back and back. Each step she took, Nicholas stepped forward, in some horrible parody of a dance.

Tarantella.

The dance to the death.

Her back touched the bookcase. She was cornered.

She raised her fists. Nicholas smiled.

"You're a lot like Claire," he said softly, almost lovingly. "She was a fighter, too." He raised his hands, a thin rope held between them.

And Professor DeLure raised his head.

Caryl jerked back in horror. She pointed. "Ni — "

"I'm not about to fall for that old trick," Nicholas grated. He lunged for her throat. The rope tightened around her neck.

Remembering a self-defense course she'd taken a lifetime ago, she fell toward Nicholas instead of away from him. Surprised, he momentarily loosened his grip, giving her a chance to slip the fingers of one hand between the noose and her throat.

The tactic gave her precious moments of air. Moments to see Professor DeLure stand up. Moments to bring up her free hand, balled into a desperate fist, and hit Nicholas as hard as she had ever hit anyone or anything in her life.

Blood spurted from Nicholas's nose. He reeled back.

"You, you, you . . ."

But he didn't finish his sentence. For now it was Nicholas whose throat was caught in a powerful grip. The dead hands of Professor DeLure closed around his neck.

Choking, fighting, Caryl fell into a sea of darkness.

Beware.

Death.

Death.

And the last thing she saw as she died was the writhing body of Nicholas France swung around like a puppet to come face to face with the corpse of Professor DeLure.

Chapter 20

"Caryl? Caryl, it's me. Dare. Speak to me."

"What about?" she croaked. Her throat was so sore. Her head hurt. The lights were too bright. She winced and closed her eyes again.

Arms tightened around her and she smelled the familiar smell of Dare's skin.

Maybe I'm not dead, she thought. Or maybe this is heaven.

The thought made her want to laugh. But it hurt to laugh.

"How is she?" A familiar voice. Professor DeLure.

"She'll be fine. We got here just in time." An unfamiliar voice, clipped and official-sounding.

Suddenly she remembered. She opened her eyes and struggled to sit up.

"Professor DeLure," she croaked. "You — you're dead!"

But he wasn't. Squinting against the throbbing of the light — or maybe it was the throbbing in her head — she could see him. He was sitting in his chair behind his desk, drinking something from a small vial and making faces like a child forced to take bad-tasting medicine.

He didn't look dead. Even as she watched, normal color began to seep back into his cheeks.

"Take it easy," said Dare.

"What happened?" Caryl asked.

"Elementary, my dear Caryl." The Professor took another sip and allowed himself the ghost of a smile. "I had long felt there was something not quite right about Nicholas. But I couldn't put my finger on it, couldn't be sure. Then when I saw the notes, and heard what was happening to you, it all fell into place.

"I knew who Nicholas was then — the madman who had kidnapped my daughter and caused her death while trying to escape with her. He had managed to get away from the institution where he was, I had thought, permanently incarcerated.

"He came here. To a madman, such a thing is logical. As was his logic in blaming someone else for Claire's death. And seeking revenge against the person he blamed."

The Professor's voice had grown low and bitter. "When I realized who he was and what his evil intent was, I decided to deal with him myself this time. To deal with him in a way that would ensure he never was able to hurt anyone again.

"Anticipating his actions, I drank a potion I'd come across in my research that induces a deathlike state, similar in some ways to what is known in certain parts of the world as 'zombie poison.' I notified the police and sat back to wait for Nicholas. But Nicholas moved almost too quickly for me, suffering as I was from the effects of the poison.

"Fortunately for you, Mr. Winters had had his own suspicions and had tracked you down here at my office. He came in, one step ahead of the police, and saved your life."

Dare shook his head. "Nicholas was so freaked out when he saw you, Professor DeLure, that I didn't have to do anything."

"You are too modest, young man." The Professor finished the contents of the vial. "The antidote," he explained with a grimace.

"Where's Nicholas? What will happen to him?" Caryl said, trying to gather her scattered wits.

"He has become catatonic," the Professor said. His voice had grown detached now, a scientist observing the outcome of an experiment. "Completely catatonic. Frozen in the position in the horrifying moment when he saw me come back to life. It is possibly a permanent state. Certainly an appropriate one."

Caryl shivered. "Poor Nicholas."

"NO!" the Professor's eyes flashed. "My only daughter is dead, the child my beloved wife entrusted to me when she died shortly after Claire was born. This monster deserves no less than what he got."

The Professor looked wildly around, then regained control of himself. He was Professor Maximillian DeLure once more: suave, smooth, unreachable. But Caryl knew, from what she had just heard and seen, that she would never see him the same way again. And maybe that was a good thing.

Professor DeLure continued smoothly, "My dear Caryl, I am more sorry than I could say for your sufferings in all this. Had I seen any other way to proceed, I would have. I hope you will forgive me."

Caryl looked at Professor DeLure. Then her eyes met Dare's.

"I forgive you," she said to the Professor at last. "But does this mean I don't belong in your writing class?"

A gleam, possibly of mirth, flashed in Professor DeLure's eye. "Spoken like a true writer, my dear. Which is what I think, given time and hard work you might certainly achieve. About your talent, I did not mislead you."

"Good," said Caryl. She leaned her head back against Dare's shoulder blissfully. She would find Anna, apologize, break the news to her. And somehow, make peace with Ben.

Maybe she'd even send Perri a get-well card.

For a moment, the vision of Giselle crossed her mind. But the vision was already fading. Soon, it would be a memory as fleeting as a dream. She would begin to wonder if it had ever been real, if she had ever stood in the entrance of Nightmare Hall and talked with a ghost. Giselle's warning had been a gift from a ghost. Perhaps the elusiveness of the memory was part of Giselle's gift, too.

She wasn't going to think about it now. For now, and maybe for a long, long time to come, she was going stay safely inside the circle of Dare's arms and not think of anything at all. Not even poetry.

"This is the hardest class I've ever taken," she said, to nobody in particular.

Dare whispered, as he leaned over, right before he kissed her. "Don't worry. You passed. You definitely passed."

Return to Nightmare Hall

. . . if you dare.

The Night Walker

Darkness. A thick curtain of soft velvety black.

Quinn Hadley stood in the door of her dorm room, arms outstretched in front of her. Her eyes were wide open. But they saw nothing.

She took one small cautious step, then another, her eyes gazing blankly out into the hallway.

Cold. Piercing cold.

Quinn shivered, clutching her thin night-gown around her.

The wandering had happened before. But she never knew . . . not until it was too late.

Silence. Not a sound.

But soon the screaming would begin.

Quinn's roommate awakened just in time to see Quinn head off down the hallway.

As if on a mission.

A deadly mission.

About the Author

"Writing tales of horror makes it hard to convince people that I'm a nice, gentle person," says **Diane Hoh**.

"So what's a nice woman like me doing scaring people?

"Discovering the fearful side of life: what makes the heart pound, the adrenalin flow, the breath catch in the throat. And hoping always that the reader is having a frightfully good time, too."

Diane Hoh grew up in Warren, Pennsylvania. Since then, she has lived in New York, Colorado, and North Carolina, before settling in Austin, Texas. "Reading and writing take up most of my life," says Hoh, "along with family, music, and gardening." Her other horror novels include *Funhouse*, *The Accident*, *The Invitation*, *The Fever*, and *The Train*.

Point Horror

Are you hooked on horror? Thrilled by fear? Then these are the books for you. A powerful series of horror fiction designed to keep you quaking in your shoes.

Point Horror

Dare you read

NIGHTMARE HALL

Where college is a
scream!

High on a hill overlooking Salem University
hidden in shadows and shrouded in mystery, sits
Nightingale Hall.

Nightmare Hall, the students call it.
Because that's where the terror began...
Don't miss the next spine-tingling thrillers:

Deadly Attraction
Guilty
Pretty Please
The Experiment
The Nightwalker
The Roommate
The Scream Team
The Silent Scream
The Wish

Now available from

Point Horror

T-shirts to make you *tremble!*

Want to be the coolest kid in the school? Then mosey on down to your local bookshop and pick up your Point Horror T-shirt and book pack.

Wear if you dare!

T-shirt and book pack available from your local bookshop now.